Vampires of Sp

Betrayed

Book 1

By
Lauree Waldrop

*Note: This book is all written and edited by the author. While I made every attempt at making perfect, it is possible that I missed a few typos. I apologize in advance.

To contact the author you may email
laureewaldrop@gmail.com

For my niece, Jesse.
Your amazing reading habits helped inspire me to
write this story. I hope you enjoy reading it as much
as I enjoyed writing it.

"Books are the quietest and most constant of friends; they are the most accessible and wisest of counselors, and the most patient of teachers."

— Charles William Eliot

CHAPTER 1

"I'll see you tomorrow." I called to my best friend Nora. We had just walked out of The Drip, a coffee shop in my small town of Splendor. Although, to be honest I'm not really sure what kind of Splendor the town has. Don't get me wrong, it's not a bad place to live but it doesn't boast anything really spectacular. I glanced back at Nora, who was headed in the opposite direction, and then stepped forward to begin my walk home. It was a warm night and even though the street was dim and deserted, I wasn't uneasy. I had made this walk so many times before. Nora and I met at The Drip for vanilla lattes every Wednesday. It was a tradition we had been observing since we got old enough to leave the house without adult supervision.

As I walked, I took in my surroundings. I had known this street for as long as I could remember; my family had lived in Splendor since the town was formed, years and years ago and my parents, like my ancestors had never wanted to live anywhere else. I took in the brick buildings that sat on either side of the street. They were old but well maintained. It gave off a historical yet elegant vibe. Come to think of it, the whole town did.

Soon, I had made it into the square which had all the businesses around the outside and a small park located in the center. I was walking past my favorite bookstore when something by the park caught my eye. I turned my attention to it and realized it was a man, leaning against one of the few old fashioned lamp posts that were situated around the square park. I looked around and didn't see anyone else. It was pretty late and the people of Splendor turn in at a decent hour. Directing my attention back to the stranger, I changed my course and started crossing the street toward him. I don't what had gotten into me; I just knew that I wanted a better look at him.

As I got closer to him the dull light from the lamp post cascaded over him and made him easy to see. He was, in a word, devastating. He had dark hair that swept over one side of his forehead and penetrating blue eyes hidden under arched and heavy brows. His jaw was strong and was preceded by high cheek bones and a full mouth that was curved into a seductive grin. His skin was a flawless alabaster. He appeared to be young but I knew he wasn't a teenager. He was tall and lean with an arrogant stance. His outfit consisted of a black leather jacket over a plain white t-shirt with a slight v neck. His dark wash jeans were well fitted hugging his rangy frame in all the appropriate places and his whole appearance had an air of sensuality edged with danger.

My stomach did a flip flop. He was the most attractive man I had ever seen. Usually, I'm not a shy girl and that night was no different. I hadn't really thought about why I was walking up to this beautiful stranger but I knew I was going to talk to him. I wanted to know him, dangerous vibe and all. I was almost to the edge of the circle of light surrounding him when he spoke.

"Nothing good happens after dark......what are you doing out so late?"

I stopped in my tracks. His voice was deep and smooth. I immediately thought that if chocolate was a sound, this would be it. I gave myself a little mental shake and replied in what I hoped was a flirty voice.

"We are the only people on this street so unless you consider yourself to be up to no good then I don't think I'll have a problem."

Geez, how lame could I be? I searched his face for his reaction. His grin grew wider and before I could blink he had disappeared from his spot against the lamp post and was standing right in front of me, not six inches from my face. I blinked a few times, trying to figure out how he had moved so quickly. He was taller than I had first assumed and I had to lean my head back to see his face. I wondered where my common sense had gone because I still wasn't afraid. I listened for warning bells in my head but I didn't hear a sound. I just looked into his dreamy blue eyes and was caught. His sapphire irises seemed to be swirling around the deep black of his pupil making them look like miniature whirlpools. Maybe it was just a trick of the light? No, they were swirling. I was sure of it.
I was turning over how strange that seemed in my mind when I heard him speak again. Only, this time the voice didn't come from his mouth. It was in my head. I was still caught in his eyes so I didn't look to see but I knew my ears weren't picking up this sound; it was just there in my brain.

"Be calm. You're not afraid. You're going to tilt your head back and offer your neck to me. What I am going to do won't hurt. Your mind will be far away. You'll be thinking about lying on a beautiful beach with clear waters and white sand. The sun will be warm on your skin and you'll be able to taste the salt in the air. When I leave you, you'll come back to yourself and not remember me at all. You didn't do anything but stop to have a day dream."

He started leaning his face in toward me and his words began to sink in. I ripped my eyes from his and caught sight of his mouth. It was open slightly and underneath the curve of his lip I saw that his canine teeth were long and razor sharp. They hadn't been like that a moment ago, I was positive. Now they didn't even look like human teeth, they looked like fangs. I was stunned for a second. How was that possible? People didn't have fangs, especially ones that appeared out of nowhere. This must be some kind of weird joke. He had learned in toward my neck so far that I couldn't see his face anymore, just the top of his head. As the reality of the situation set in, a light bulb went on in my head. Joke or not, it wasn't funny anymore and his close proximity had finally set off alarm bells. I screamed and pushed at him with both hands. He didn't budge an inch. I stepped backwards furiously, still pushing at him. It didn't do me any good. I probably would have had better luck pushing a concrete wall. I was halfway into turning to run when his arms shot out and his hands gripped me, one on each of my biceps. His grip was like stone. With what appeared to be no effort at all, he drug me forward against his body and wrapped his arms around me in a bear hug, locking my arms in between our bodies. I couldn't see his face but I heard him mutter some curse words and I felt one of his hands run up my back and tangle painfully in my hair. I was still trying to struggle by kicking my feet and pushing against his chest with my arms but it didn't have an effect on him and I was beginning to run out of steam. He didn't seem to notice any of my efforts as he pulled my head back by a fistful of hair and leaned his face down to the side of my throat. I could feel his hot breath on my skin and I broke out in goose bumps. I felt his mouth on my neck and for a vague moment wondered if he was kissing me. Then I felt his teeth sink into my skin. It was a sharp concentrated pain that seemed to travel throughout my whole body with lightning speed. I jerked and gave one last attempt at shoving him away. His only response was to move his face away a fraction and squeeze me even tighter until I was completely immobile. I gave up struggling...all I was doing was wearing myself out and all his squeezing was making it hard for me to breathe. I was going to try to talk to him, maybe reason with him but then I felt the blood that was gushing out of my throat and running down my chest to spill over my clothes. In the corner of my mind, I had the thought that my white shirt was going to be ruined; I'd only worn it twice! Pushing that away, I felt his lips on my neck again. What was he doing? Why would he put his mouth on my bloody throat? Better yet, how crazy was he to bite me in the first place? Then I heard the slurping sound. His lips and tongue were mushing into my skin and I could hear and feel the suction as he slurped my blood into his mouth. Any thought I had entertained about talking this guy into letting me go left my mind in a quick flash. He was obviously nuts. Normal people didn't go around drinking (and I was sure he was drinking because I could hear him swallowing) other people's blood. As he drank, I started to feel light headed. With a sigh, I resigned myself to the fact that I wasn't going to get out of this. I wondered if he would kill me...that seemed

9

the most likely scenario. My thoughts started to slow down and my brain turned sluggish but I realized he was a vampire. I knew they weren't real but somewhere deep down inside of me I was, without a doubt, positive that that was the answer. Before I could think about it any further, my vision went black and I drifted away.

CHAPTER 2

I came back into my mind slowly. I just kind of drifted into it. One minute there was nothing and the next I could feel the heavy weight of my body. The first thing that registered with me was that my mom was talking to me. Her voice was faint but rapidly got louder until I knew she was right next to me. I felt a warm hand slide over mine and I knew it must be hers. The second thing I realized was that I felt like I had been run over by a Peterbilt. There was an ache in all of my bones and it radiated from within them coming to an end humming over my skin. Worse than that, was the fire burning in my neck, which intensified with every breath I took. I pushed the pain away and opened my eyes. This was a monumental effort since they were swollen and crusted shut. As I opened them, my vision was filled with blinding light. I blinked a few times encouraging them to adjust. My eye lids felt scratchy and the light was painful. Everything started to clear and I could see my mom leaned over me. I could tell she had been crying. Her eyes were puffy and there were streaks of mascara down her cheeks but her expression was happy. Confused, I stared at her blankly.

Tentatively she spoke "Sophie? Sophie honey, can you answer me?"

It took me a minute to make my voice work and it came out dry and scratchy. "Yea mom, where am I?"

My mom's face went from happy to beaming.

"The hospital. I am so glad you're awake. Now I can really believe you are going to be okay. The other night after you went to meet Nora, you didn't come home and I got worried. I called Nora and when she said you should have already been home, I drove the route you would have taken and found you on the sidewalk. You'd lost a lot of blood. The police think you were attacked by a wild animal....maybe a dog. Do you remember any of that?"

My brain was still cloudy and it took me a minute to process what she had said but I tried to revive the memory. I was almost ready to give up and tell my mom I had no recollection of any of it when it all flooded back. I had been attacked but not by an animal, it was by the most physically appealing man I had ever seen. Sickening inside, I also remembered him drinking my blood. Yuck! My epiphany during the attack came back to me as well and my head spun while I wrapped my mind around it. I had been attacked by a vampire. I sounded crazy, even to myself but I knew that's what he was. It was impossible for a human to do the things I had witnessed him do. The super quick movements, the incredible strength, the fangs....it all added up to something supernatural and with the blood drinking the only answer was that he was a vampire. I wanted to shake my head and say I was wrong but somehow I couldn't. I think in black and white most of the time. Something either is or isn't, there isn't much middle ground with me. I knew I could debate the matter but why waste time doing so when I knew what I had seen and no amount of inner turmoil was going to change that. I took a deep breath and just accepted it. Vampires existed. Wow. Honestly, I was fascinated. Don't get me wrong, I was not thrilled that I had been someone's dinner but the whole idea of something so mystical being fact and not fiction was pretty engrossing.

Shaking myself out of my revelation, I looked at my mom, who was waiting for my answer with a questioning look. I might have been ready to admit I was attacked by a vampire but I was definitely not ready to have my mom and everyone else call me crazy. I took a deep breath (ouch!) and spoke in my still raspy voice.

"No, I don't remember. It all goes kind of blank after I got to The Drip. How long have I been here?"

"Almost a day and a half. They told me you'd recover not long after you were admitted but they said it might take a while for you to wake up since you had lost so much blood and needed a transfusion."

Maybe my mind was still a little groggy because my first reaction to her words was to be really creeped out. They had pumped me full of someone else's blood? Ew! Though, given the alternative of dying, I was glad to accept. I couldn't really think of anything else to say to her because my head was pretty hectic trying to absorb it all. Fortunately, she decided to go find the doctor and see if she would come in and take a look at me. When she had left and shut the door behind her I found the control and elevated the hospital bed to a sitting position, it was painful but I wanted a look around. I briefly surveyed my surroundings. It was a typical hospital room complete with ugly mauve wallpaper, framed generic landscapes and the smell of cleaner. Uninterested in the room, I turned my mind back to my newfound knowledge. What was I going to do about it? At this point, nothing. I could tell someone but I wasn't naïve enough to think they wouldn't instantly cart me off to a psychiatrist who would ask me questions about my child hood and scribble notes while pretending to understand. (I've never been to a psychiatrist but I visualized that's how it would be) Of course, if someone had told me vampires existed a few days before I probably would have had them carted off too.

Before I could ask myself any more questions, I heard a gentle knock on my door. Thinking it was probably my mom, I invited the visitor in. For the second time in two days, I was looking at a gorgeous stranger (The first one was definitely something out of a horror movie but I could still admit he was hot). My visitor had chestnut hair that waved and curled over his ears slightly and a wide and sensuous mouth that was currently set in a firm and serious line. His eyes were a deep gray that resembled clouds before a storm. He wore a plain and collared white button up shirt with the sleeves rolled to elbow and the neck hanging open. His distressed jeans were a faded blue and neither baggy nor constricting. I was feeling awful but I couldn't help but appreciate the view. When he came to stand at the foot of my hospital bed, I recovered my wits enough to speak.

"Who are you?"

His expression was unreadable as he replied in a voice that had a slight musical quality to it.

"My name is Lucas. I was wondering if you could tell me what attacked you."

I gave him points for being direct.

"Well...um...I think it was a...a vampire." I had no idea what possessed me to tell him the truth, it just sort of tumbled out.

He stood there for a minute not moving. The silence was distressing. "So do you think I am crazy or what?"

"No. I believe you."

I hadn't been expecting any response besides "yes".

"Okay...." My voice trailed off. I wasn't sure what to say. You could almost see the tension in the room.

After a moment he walked around to the side of my bed and bent down to take my hand. I looked into his eyes and noticed they were swirling in a scary and familiar way. Before I could decide on the best way to react, I heard his voice in my head. It was like déjà vu. Nothing was coming out of his mouth and I wasn't picking up sound with my ears, his voice was just there among my thoughts.

"What you saw was real but now you have to forget it. You don't remember anything about your attack."

When his words started to sink in, I pulled my eyes from his and pushed his hand away. He gave me a confused look and backed up a few steps. I tried to make my voice as clear as possible.

"What are you talking about? I didn't forget I remember exactly what happened. WHO ARE YOU?"

I saw a discontented look pass quickly over his face and then it was replaced with calm determination. He leaned forward a little but didn't make a move to touch me. His voice was low and steady.

"I am not going to harm you Sophie. Please trust me on that, I'm also sorry I upset you, that wasn't my intention. I know you are confused and there are things you don't understand but I cannot explain them right now. I have one request and then I will leave you to get some rest....Sophie...do not under any circumstances tell anyone about your attack. If they ask say you don't remember. This is very important. Can you do that for me?"
"Will you explain all of this to me if I agree not to say anything?"

He answered quickly. "Yes, I'll explain it all but not today."

I slowly nodded.

He turned to walk away and I called to him "How do I find you?"

He called back over his shoulder "You don't, I'll find you" and he gently shut the door behind him.

Alone again, I took record of my situation. One- Vampires were real. Two- I had been attacked by one and was pretty sure I had met another, all in less than 48 hours. Three- They were both gorgeous.

The door to my room swung open. I was tensed not knowing who to expect when Nora and my mom walked in. They both had big smiles and Nora let out a squeal and flung her arms around me.

"Yay! You're awake! Don't ever scare me like that again"

I contorted in pain and she let me go quickly. Before she could apologize or I could respond, my mom cut in.

"I wanted to let you know that the sheriff will be by later. He wants to talk to you about your attack. They want to get this animal off the street before it hurts someone else. I know you said you don't remember and I know it will be awful but could you try to recall something? They can use any clues you might be able to give them."

With a nod, I silently added to the list in my head. Four- I was going to spend the rest of the day lying to everyone. I groaned…It was going to be a long day.

CHAPTER 3

I sat at my white-painted wooden vanity and stared at my reflection in the mirror. My eyes scanned the heart shaped face staring back at me. It had large, almond shaped, sage green eyes set under subtle eyebrows. The nose was rounded and small and the mouth was full and pouty. All of my features were surrounded by a cascade of straight, long, golden blond hair. I stood to scrutinize the rest of me. I am average height and slender while still having curves. I was wearing dark skinny jeans tucked into flat heeled boots and a billowy, emerald silk tunic. I had kept my jewelry minimal by only wearing some diamond stud earrings that had been a birthday gift from my mom. I looked like my usual self other than the large bandage taped to the side of my neck. I knew the bandage hid a row of stitches. It wasn't what I had been expecting the first time I had cautiously peeled away the gauze to survey the damage. I had been prepared to see cliché fang marks but instead I had been confronted with a line of large stitches. My mother had explained that before it was stitched up it had only been a large gaping hole, just like something had bitten a large chunk out of my throat. A shiver passed through me and I pushed those thoughts away.

I was getting ready to go back to school after being out for a week. I felt so different on the inside, that I had look in the mirror and double check to make sure everything on the outside was still normal- I figured being attacked and learning vampires existed would do that you.

Leaving the mirror I went around my room gathering my stuff for school. My room was tidy and my bed was habitually made. Other than that I guessed it was a typical room for an 18 year old girl. All my furniture was painted white wood and I'd had it since my childhood. The comforter that covered my bed was red with white polka dots and the curtains on the single window in the room matched. There was a desk and a vanity along with a tall chest of drawers. The walls were white and unembellished except for some frames that held my favorite photos of family and friends. My bathroom adjoined by a door to the side.

Sweeping my eyes over the room to be sure I hadn't forgotten anything I tried to shake off the apprehension I was feeling. I knew the day would be filled with people asking me how I felt and what happened and I wasn't ready to talk. I hadn't even told Nora the truth. Since the first day I woke up in the hospital she had been with me or calling regularly to check up on me. It was draining to hold back the truth and I didn't think adding people to that list would help assuage the guilt I was feeling.

I headed downstairs to the kitchen, when I reached the doorway I saw my mom and my little sister Bailey sitting at the round table that filled the dining area. My mom had a mug of coffee in her hands and was leaned against the back of her chair while Bailey was animatedly telling her how excited she was for her class field trip to a local wildlife preserve . Mom nodded at appropriate intervals and wore an interested expression. I took in the contrast between them. My mother shared her blond hair and green eyes with me but Bailey had the dark features of my father. Her hair was so dark it was almost black and her eyes were soulful brown. Being reminded of him was painful for me and I could feel the pangs in my chest. He had died a year before in a car accident and I missed him with a ferocity that I hadn't known was possible. I knew my mom and Bailey missed him too but we had finally managed to piece together a routine without him. Pushing thoughts of him away, I walked in and stooped to give Bailey a smacking kiss on the cheek and a tummy tickle that sent the little girl into a fit of giggles. Bailey was only six years old, a big gap from my eighteen but I adored her. My mom watched us, smiling at our exchange. When I moved over to the cabinets to grab a toaster pastry she spoke.

"Morning Soph. How are you feeling?"

"I'm fine just ready to get back to normal and get started on the mountain of make-up work I'm sure is waiting for me".

Her eyes were sympathetic when she said "Are you sure? You could wait a few more days if you want."

I appreciated her concern but I knew the longer I put it off the more I was going to dread it. "Yea, I'm sure."

She smiled at me, obviously proud of my determination. She grabbed her coffee mug off the table and walked by me to drop it in the sink. She gave me a quick hug.

"Okay hun, as long as you are sure. I'm off to get Bailey to school and head to work. Have a good day. Love you!"

"Love you too mom!" I said as I watched her gather up her purse and Bailey and walk out the door. I poured myself some coffee and sat down at the table. My mom had painted the kitchen an azure blue and added new appliances a few years before but the dining table and chairs had been around longer than I had. It was comforting to sit in the same spot I had sat at for years. It helped take my mind off my dread for the upcoming day. After finishing my breakfast, I locked up the house and walked out to my car.

I drove a black, five year old Ford Explorer. Originally, it had been my mom's but the year I turned 16 she had bought a brand new car and passed hers down to me. I liked my car and was happy to have it especially, when I thought of how many of my friends had to buy their own. Some people thought I was spoiled and maybe I was a little but I appreciated everything my parents had ever done for me and I tried to earn it all by being sure to obey their rules and get good grades.

On the way to school my mind wandered to Lucas. I hadn't heard from him since I saw him at the hospital and I had doubts on if I ever would. Perhaps he only said he'd explain to convince me to keep my attack a secret. I had bitten the bullet and accepted that vampires existed rather than trying to argue with myself over what I knew I had seen but I couldn't make up my mind on Lucas. I was pretty sure he was a vampire too; the similarities between him and the one I had met were too significant to ignore. I was having a hard time believing that a normal human has the power of telepathic communication. On the other hand, he didn't assault me and leave me for dead. Somehow I felt like I could trust him and I knew I had to have some answers, so I still hoped he would find me. When I pulled into the parking lot of Splendor High School I turned all my energy to making it through the day.

The morning went by quickly and was just what I had expected, a lot of people wishing me well and asking questions. Plus, I had an overload of work that I had missed. By the time lunch rolled around I was feeling pretty sour. I was standing in the outdoor courtyard when Nora called to me. I waved in response and she headed my direction. Nora arrived at my side with a natural smile that reached all the way to her honey colored eyes that were set off by her shock of curly red hair.

"Hey you! How were classes?" Nora said beaming in her usual manner.

"Fine, a mountain of make-up work as expected". My voice sounded bleak.

"Oh don't you go all Eeyore on me; you have an A in every class. It won't take you long to finish it all....besides it's almost the end of senior year. We'll be graduating in a few months so loosen up and have fun! Do hear me missy?" Nora replied still smiling and unfazed by my morose expression.

"Yes ma'am" I answered with a giggle and a pretend salute. Nora never failed to put a smile on my face.

Nodding to show her approval over my shift in mood, Nora spoke again "Well you always have me for moral support! When you finish it all we can reward ourselves with a girl's night complete with chocolate and chic flicks!"

I laughed "I'm the one doing all the make-up work. Why do you get rewarded?"

"Because you wouldn't enjoy it without my exceptional company" Nora said in an sarcastic, dramatic voice. We burst into giggles simultaneously.

Nora recovered first, her tone conspiratorial. "On a more serious note...have you seen the new guy?"

"New guy?" I gave her a quizzical look.

Nora continued "Yep there is a new student. He was in my economics class this morning. I am surprised you haven't heard...all the girls are talking about him. Not that I blame them, he's a total babe!"

I sniggered a little at her announcement. Nora could be very crass and I couldn't help but love her for it.
Nora looked over my shoulder, her face turned beet red and I heard a throat clear behind me. Turning around sluggishly, I found myself face to face with Lucas. I quickly deduced that he was the new guy. I hadn't exaggerated his appeal in my memory-neither had Nora.

23

He was eyeing me with an indecipherable expression but his voice was welcoming.

"Pardon my interruption....I just wanted say hello to Sophie."

Nora looked at him with a guarded expression and then flicked her eyes to me. "You two know each other?"

I was rummaging my brain for an answer when Lucas intervened.

"Yes, we met at the hospital. I was visiting a relative and entered Sophie's room by mistake."

Nora didn't look mollified but she slowly nodded. There was a moment of uncomfortable silence and then the bell rang signaling the end of lunch period. Nora gave me an expression that told me I was going to have serious explaining to do later and headed to class with a wave. Lucas and I stood immobile and silent as the courtyard slowly emptied. When there were only a few other students milling around, I looked at him and spoke keeping my voice low. I didn't want to be overheard. "Are you here to tell me what I want to know or are you just going to leave me with a questions again?"

I was sure there had been sarcasm in my tone but he either didn't notice or ignored it.

"I am here to explain. However, I don't think this is really the best place to do that. Would you mind leaving and going somewhere with me so that we can speak freely?"

I turned the offer over in my brain. I shouldn't skip school and definitely not with a stranger that I was pretty sure could be deadly if he wanted. Then again, if my suspicions were right and he wanted to kill me, I'd already be dead. A quote I had heard somewhere ran through my mind.

"When you look back on your life you'll regret the things you didn't do more than the ones you did."

My decision was made. Lucas stood holding his hand out, waiting to see what I would do. Without hesitation, I put my hand in his.

We walked to the parking lot in silence and I took the opportunity to marvel over the coolness of his hand in mine. He led me to an electric blue Mustang. He opened the door for me and I slid into the seat. My heart was hammering as he walked around and climbed into the other side. I was nervous and my whole body was on edge. As he was pulling out of the parking lot I tried to break the silence.

"Now will you..."

"Be patient we aren't driving far and as soon as we get there I swear I'll explain everything and answer your questions"

I huffed and slumped back in my seat. I kept my face turned toward the window to avoid staring at him. Trapped in such close quarters I picked up on something I hadn't noticed before; His smell. It was like a mixture of clean linens and mint. It was enticing. I tried to block it out and remember that I

25

was there for answers, nothing more. A few silent minutes later Lucas turned off the road into the parking lot of a small nature reserve, it wasn't much other than a diminutive wood with walking trails cut through it. I had been there countless times. It was a place to come when I needed to think out a problem. As we got out of the car I broke the silence between us.

"The reserve? What are we doing here?"

"I like to walk and it's peaceful. Plus we needed a place to talk without being disturbed and since it's the middle of a week day no one will be here." He answered as he headed toward the nearest trail.

Before I could reconsider my decision I hurried after him. "I come here to think sometimes, when I have a problem I need to figure out."

I hadn't really meant to tell him that but Lucas nodded understandingly. We had reached the trail and made it a few yards into the trees before he spoke.

"Everything I am about to tell you is going to change how you see the world. I would ask you if you are ready for that but since I've met you, you have been determined to get answers out of me and I don't think you'll change your mind now."

I didn't speak but I slowly nodded.

"I believe your story about how you were attacked, and you were right when you said it was a vampire. I know people think they are just myths and only exist in movies and books but they are real."

I suppressed a little gasp. I had accepted the inevitable as soon as I realized how I had been attacked but it is still a little discomforting to have it confirmed by someone else.

"I don't know who attacked you but I know what he was. I came to the hospital because I read about your attack in the paper and I suspected it was a lot more than an animal. After talking to you my suspicions were confirmed. I am sorry I have kept you waiting for answers but truthfully I wasn't sure if I should tell you and there hasn't been an appropriate time or place until now. I know you picked up on my.....oddities at the hospital and you seem clever enough to put two and two together but I am a vampire."

He hesitated and looked at me expectantly. I felt a tremor of fear but I kept quiet and gave him an encouraging look. His voice was calm when he continued.

"Please don't be afraid. I don't feed off of humans. Some of the books and movies got that part right. I buy blood bags from a few special sources or I can drink animal blood when I am in a pinch. I didn't choose to be a monster so I try my best not to live like one."

When he stopped, I held my face in a blank expression and waited a few beats to see if he would continue. When he didn't, I took it as my cue and asked the first thing that came to mind.

"I thought vampires couldn't walk around in the sunlight. How come you can?"

He chuckled almost imperceptibly and put his hands in his pockets. He was more relaxed than I had ever seen him.

"That's a myth. I'm not positive on how it got started but I would imagine it came around because most vampires live a nocturnal lifestyle by choice. It's much easier to feed during night hours; there are less people around to notice and we have excellent night vision so the darkness is not a problem"

I tuned out thoughts of people being preyed on in the night and proceeded.

"Can you die?"

He raised an eyebrow in what I assumed was surprise.

"Yes I can die but not on my own. I can't get sick or grow old. The only way for me to die is by a stake to the heart or decapitation. Another myth that is actually a fact."

The subject of decapitation was a little bizarre for me so I moved on.

"Okay...umm how did I hear you in my head?" I waited with held breath. He never actually confirmed that I had heard him in my mind. I was curious about how he would answer.

"I was trying to enthrall you. Vampires have the power to control your mind. I thought if you didn't remember your attack that it would be better for both of us. I'm not sure why but it didn't work. I have never met a human who could resist it."

Well. That certainly gave me something to think on later. I fumbled around for the right words to ask my next question and then spit them out quickly.

"How did you become a vampire?"

I squeezed my eyes shut and waited for his response. I didn't know if that counted as a personal question and I didn't savor the idea of upsetting him. Sneaking a peek, I saw him glance over at me quickly and I was sure I had asked the wrong question but then he began speaking, his voice placid.

"In 1901, I was twenty-one years old and living in South Carolina with my parents on the farm where I grew up. One evening my sister Emily and I were walking home from visiting a sick neighbor. As we neared our home a man came out of the darkness and attacked us. I awoke three days later in a ramshackle cabin in the middle of a large wood. I couldn't remember much about the encounter but I quickly realized that I was not the same. Not knowing where else to go, I went home and watched my parents through the window. From listening to them, I found out that when Emily and I had not returned home, they set out to search for us. They found the spot where we had been attacked and saw the blood in the road. They assumed we were dead. I knew I couldn't go back home, I had heard tales from men in town about vampires and I knew that's what I had to be. I couldn't mistake my thirst for blood and lack of pulse. I searched all around for Emily but all I found were the clothes she had been wearing and large amounts of blood. I first believed that she may have been turned like me but I am certain Emily wouldn't have left without finding me so I knew she must be dead. After my search came up bare I left South Carolina and wandered from town to town. I was a monster in every sense of the word. I killed many people, it was impossible to control my urges for blood. Eventually, I would come across others like me and I would learn more about myself. When I learned I could survive on animal blood and blood bags became available, I decided I didn't want to feed on people any more. It weighed heavily on my conscience and I had developed a much better control over my thirst. After wandering for so long, I decided to find a place to settle down for a while. I can live above suspicion fairly easy now and I want to try to have a life that resembles ordinary. I know I'll never get my human life back but I hope to get close. I have passed through Splendor a few times over the years and I like the peace it seems to have, so now I am here for a while. I have rented a house and am telling everyone that I am eighteen years old and the recipient of a large inheritance from recently deceased parents. It allows me to go to high school and keeps people from asking why I have no parents and how I afford things."

As he finished his story with a voice heavy with guilt, I was teary eyed. I had felt a few trickles of fear since I had stepped into the woods alone with him but as he told me his story they simply vanished. All I felt for him was compassion. It must have been terrible for him. His being a vampire had fascinated me but now I was fascinated by him. Something appalling had happened to him and yet he was able to overcome it. I knew it was wrong that he had killed people but he hadn't done it out of hate or rage it was part of what he had become and he seemed to be paying for it with enough guilt to convince him to try to abstain. I surveyed his face as we walked but he had his eyes on the ground and I couldn't decipher his expression. Not really knowing what to say I spoke softly.

"I am sorry."

He peered over at me and met my watery eyes. He appeared surprised for a second and then he smiled.

"Thank you Sophie. When I told you my story I wasn't expecting you to feel anything other than disgust for me and what I have done, your sympathy is touching. The lives I have taken are a burden to me but I cannot help but to be grateful to you for thinking of me."

The conversation had gotten very depressing. I decided to move it along with more questions. I asked everything that I could possibly think of and he gave me a detailed answer for each one. I guess some of my questions seemed pretty ridiculous to him since I was pulling information from every vampire movie and book I could remember. Yet, he never made me feel foolish. When I asked him if he sparkled he let out a large laugh and told me that he definitely didn't. I learned that he could move faster than I could comprehend and that his hearing and eyesight were far better than mine. He could also fly but he said it was more like floating.

I never imagined that I would walk through the woods with a vampire and that it would be enjoyable but that's exactly what I did. He was easy to talk to and vampire or not, he was very charming. I was at ease with him. By the time we approached the end of the trail I was walking at an easy pace and feeling very relaxed. He had given me a lot to think about but none of it seemed to be too much to handle. The light atmosphere between us continued all the way back to the school. We reached my car right after classes had let out and only a few cars remained in the parking lot. Lucas parked and followed me out of his car. We stood face to face for an awkward minute and then he spoke. His voice was somber.

"Sophie, I am glad that I told you everything and you have taken it far better than I expected but you need to understand that you can't tell anyone. Other vampires are not like me, if they find out what you know they won't hesitate to kill you to keep our secret safe."

I gulped a little but stared into his stormy eyes to answer.

"I have no intentions of telling anyone. I believe what you say and I'm not stupid enough to

32

think blabbing to everyone I know wouldn't put them or myself in danger. Not to mention, I may be sure your telling me the truth but no one else would believe me if I told them. They would think I had lost my mind."

His mouth curved up in an alluring smile.
"I should have known. I hope that we can be friends after all this. I understand if you don't want that but it's refreshing to be around someone who knows what I am and doesn't seem to mind."

"Lucas, of course we are friends. I don't care that you're a vampire. You seem to have the whole bloodlust thing under control and I believe you when you say that you won't hurt me. Honestly, it's not like I can talk about this with anyone else and I extremely doubt that I am going to be able to forget about it and pretend it never happened so I have no intention of trying."

He smiled and nodded. I looked up at him and waited; I wasn't really sure how I should conclude a day out with a vampire. His face took on a peaceful image and he leaned on toward me. I froze and closed my eyes. I felt cool firm lips brush against my cheek bone and then he was gone. I opened my eyes and smiled at him as he got into his car. My cheek was still tingling when he drove off.

CHAPTER 4

A few surreal days after my afternoon with Lucas, I sat at the drip having coffee with Nora. Over a week had passed since I had been attacked, and I had pushed the memory of it away. Lucas and I had started an easygoing friendship and it seemed to occupy the forefront of my mind. He had taken to spending his lunch period with Nora and me, as well as walking me to my classes. His allure had only increased and I genuinely enjoyed his company.

"Sophie?! Earth to Sophie!" I pulled myself from my thoughts and looked at Nora. She was staring at me with quizzical eyes.

"Sorry." My apology came out in a mumble.

"What is with you lately? You always seem to be out in space. Whenever I ask if it's because of the attack you brush me off and tell me you're fine. I know there is something on your mind. Now, spill it!"

Nora's had crossed her arms and was wearing her determined face. I should have known I couldn't keep my best friend completely in the dark. I couldn't tell her the truth and I struggled for a second trying to find the right thing to say. I decided to stick to the truth as much as I could.

"I'm sorry. It's not about the attack. I guess I am just confused over Lucas. I am definitely attracted to him but I don't know if he feels the same."

I sighed in relief. I hadn't lied to her, everything I said was true. I just left out some extra details, like the fact that Lucas was a vampire and that was the main reason I was hesitant over my feelings for him.
Her posture relaxed and her mouth twisted into a devilish grin.

"Well, why didn't you say something? I can answer that question, easily! Of course, he feels the same! He's by your side every free moment at school and when you talk he hangs on your every word."

"I don't know Nora. Maybe he is just a really nice guy and is just trying to make friends."

"Sophie, he gives you THE look! Guys don't give you THE look if all they want is to be friends."

I could see that Nora was really enjoying this conversation. She sees analyzing men's behavior as her forte.

"I am almost afraid to ask, but what look are you referring to?"

"Ugh! Sophie, you can be very dense sometimes! THE look! The one that says I'm really into you and I am hoping you'll make the first move all while he simultaneously pictures doing the deed with you."

"Nora!" I couldn't help but smile at her quick and to the point reflection, even if I didn't wholly agree with it. "Might I ask exactly how you came up with this brilliant conclusion?"

She shrugged and gave me a wicked smirk. "It's a gift."

Still smiling, I decided it was time to rain on her parade. "Maybe your right and he is interested in me but I am definitely not 'doing the deed with him'. I don't even know if I want to date him!"

Her grin didn't falter. "I don't expect you to. You haven't 'done the deed' with anyone and I'm not suggesting you run off to do it with him simply because he is in to you but it doesn't change the fact that he has thought about it. He is a man."

I let out a chuckle because I could always trust Nora to be honest to a fault. Eager to change the subject, I asked her about an English essay we had been assigned earlier in the day. We were supposed to write about Hester's portrayal of puritan values in *The Scarlet Letter* and the topic took up the rest of our visit. When we realized it had gotten late Nora and I made our way out to the parking lot. We used to walk but given the events of my last walk we decided driving was healthier. We said goodbye and I gave her a wave as I slid into the driver's seat of my car. As I was turning the key to crank my Explorer, something on the dash caught my eye. I flipped on the interior light to inspect it. It was a pink rose with perfectly shaped petals. I lifted it from the dash and brought it to me nose to inhale its sweet scent. I had no idea why someone would give me a rose so I searched the dash for a note or clue to explain its presence but I came up with nothing. Puzzled, I cranked my car and headed home, all the while wondering who the rose had come from.

The next morning as I pulled into the parking lot of school I searched for Lucas. I backed into a parking spot and before I could shut off the engine, I spotted him walking toward me with a smile on his face. I quickly gathered my stuff and stepped out to greet him.
"Hey!"

I took in his outfit for today. He was wearing blue and white plaid shorts with a matching blue polo shirt that lent his gray eyes a bluish hue and he was sporting his usual boyish grin.

"Good Morning Sophie."

"You know, I'm amazed by how well you blend in. No one would ever guess that you've been around over a hundred years" I looked around as I spoke making sure there was no one nearby to overhear.

He let out a sly chuckle.
"I'll take that as a compliment. I have gotten very good at adapting and if I am being honest, I enjoy modern clothing. It's comfortable and much more practical."

"I'll take your word for it. You ready to head to class?"

"Sure."

As we walked side by side toward the building, I debated on the rose from the night before. I was at a loss on who had placed it in my car but part of me was hoping it had been him. He had kissed me on the cheek the day he revealed his big secret to me but he hadn't done anything else to signal more than a friendship between us. I admitted to myself that I was hoping for more. After a moment I gave up on finding a delicate way to bring it up and decided to ask him outright.

"I wanted to ask you about something. It might sound strange but I want to check anyways. After coffee with Nora last night, I found a rose in my car. I don't know who put it there and I was wondering if it might have been you."

"No, I didn't put it there but why would it be strange to ask me about it?"

His face was genuinely puzzled.
I twirled my hands in front of me nervously.

"Well... we're just friends and I didn't want you to think I was reading too much into it."

We had entered the building and reached the door of my first class. We both stopped and turned to each other. His eyes flickered with amusement as he responded.

"A friendship is never turned into something more unless someone 'reads too much into it' "

He turned and strolled away. I rushed into class and spent the rest of the period speculating on the meaning of his cryptic remark.

Throughout the day Lucas walked me to my classes and spent lunch period with Nora and I but he didn't mention our conversation from that morning and I didn't bring it up either. When the final bell rang I walked to my car absorbed in my thought. When I arrived I noticed Lucas standing a few feet away. He came and took my books from me as he spoke.

"Do you want to come to my house today? I thought we could work on our English papers together."

"You need help with your paper?"

He let out a quiet snicker "No. I just wanted a reason for us to spend time together."

He wanted to spend time with me; I took it as a good sign. "Okay. Do you want me to follow you there?"

"That sounds good. I'll see you in a few minutes then"

He had put my books in my backseat as he spoke. With that done, he trotted off toward his car and I couldn't help but notice that his rear view was just as good as his front. I sighed in appreciation as I turned and hopped into my car. When Lucas had pulled out of his parking spot he stopped and waited for me to pull up behind him. From there I followed him on a short drive to the edge of town, where he turned into a gravel driveway that I had never noticed before even though I had traveled the road many times. The driveway was long and led us into a grouping of trees before opening up to an expansive lawn. I pulled up to the house behind Lucas and sat slack jawed for a moment. I had spent the drive wondering about what his house would look like. Of all the things I had imagined it wasn't anything like the house before me. It was a federal style brick house with two large white columns on each side of a dark wooden door. There was a wide semi-circle of stairs leading to the entrance and centered above it all was a balcony with an ornate railing and a door leading into the second story. It was topped off with a chimney on each side of the roof. I gave myself a quick mental shake, grabbed my books and climbed out of my car to meet Lucas who was already waiting for me a few feet from the stairs.

"What do you think?" he asked me with a grin.

"It's beautiful! You might be able to dress so you blend in but this house is over the top." I said teasing.

He chuckled. "I have a weakness for fine homes. It is one of the indulgences I have allowed myself since I decided to settle down. Before I came here I was always moving and it just wasn't practical to own a home like this."

"I know it's none of my business but how can you afford this?" I couldn't contain my curiosity as we made our way up the stairs to the door.

"Over the years, I have made some very smart financial investments, so smart that I can

41

afford to live very comfortably." He said this without any hint of cockiness, it was just a statement.

He turned his head to give me an inviting look as he pushed open the front door. He put out a hand, gesturing for me to go in first. I stepped into the foyer and looked around. There were beautiful wooden floors and the walls were painted soothing sea foam green. There were doorways on each side of the foyer as well as a hallway leading to the back of the house and a stair case that led up to a landing and what I assumed to be more rooms. I realized that there were detailed landscape paintings on the walls. Taking it all in, I felt like I had stepped back in time. I turned to face Lucas who had stepped in after me and closed the door behind him.

"It's gorgeous. I feel like I should be wearing a Scarlet O'Hara dress."

"You fit in perfectly just the way you are. Would you like to see the rest of it?"

"Yes!" I was unable to curb my enthusiasm.

He crooked his elbow in my direction and I walked up and slid my arm through it. I let out a giggle. As modern as he was, every now and then he would do something to reveal his true age. He led me into the first room off of the foyer and beamed when my eyes grew wide. It was set up to be a living room and was painted a deep red. The furniture was Victorian style and all the fabrics were deep jewel tones. It was stunning and in a peculiar way it was very masculine and very Lucas. At his urging, I placed my books on one of the two teal sofas in the room and he led me on through the rest of the downstairs and each room was as beautiful as the next. He smiled approvingly at my reactions but he didn't offer to take me upstairs and not wanting to invade his privacy, I didn't ask to see it. Not seeing it downstairs, I knew his bedroom must be up there. I wondered if he slept in a coffin but quickly shut away the idea. He didn't fit in with any of the vampire stereotypes created by books and movies and I couldn't imagine there was anything practical about it, so it didn't seem very likely. When we made our way back to the living room, he suggested working on our English papers there. I sat down on the sofa next to my stuff and was reaching for my English book when he spoke.

"I don't usually keep food in the house but can I get you something to drink? I keep a stock of bottled water and soda for guests."

"A soda would be great." I paused for a moment. "Can you drink soda? I've never seen you eat or drink anything."

"I could drink or eat human food if I wanted to but I rarely do. My body doesn't have a need for it and I don't find the taste of it very appealing."

"How often do you have to...feed?" I wasn't sure if the question counted as rude but I was too interested in the answer to care.

"It's best if I consume at least a small amount a day but I could sustain by feeding once a week or so." He answered my question without hesitation and didn't seem to mind my prying.

"When do you normally feed?" Fascinated, I continued my questioning.

His voice came out low and a little apprehensive. "Actually, I usually feed about this time but since you are here I'll wait until later tonight."

"If I am the only thing stopping you, go ahead. It won't bother me." I spoke before I could really think about it. It was kind of creepy to think about him drinking blood in front of me but I understood that he needed it to survive and I was also morbidly curious about what he looked like when he fed. Maybe his forehead bulged out or his eyes turned red. He cocked one of his eyebrows in question and I thought he would refuse but his only verbal response was "Okay."

He turned and walked toward the door that I knew from the tour led to a small but elegantly decorated and surprisingly modern kitchen. I turned my attention to finding the proper page in my

English book and when I found it, I looked around vacantly, waiting for him to come back. Suddenly, I felt a cool rush of air and he was standing right beside me. He grinned at my openly shocked face as he handed me a cold soda, still in the can. I reached and took it from him robotically, stunned by his quick entrance. In another second he was sitting on the sofa opposite of the one I was perched on. I had witnessed vamp speed during my encounter with the first one I met but it had been hard to comprehend at the time, seeing Lucas move so quickly was fascinating as well as a little unnerving. I studied him as I popped the tab on my soda. He was reclined comfortably on the couch and was holding an oversized opaque blue mug in one hand. I was staring and I couldn't help it. I knew there was blood in that cup and I was waiting for him to take a drink. He looked at me with as if he knew my thoughts and then lifted the cup to his lips to take a large sip. His eyes hadn't left mine as he brought the cup back down. I scanned his face but didn't notice anything unusual until he smiled. His teeth were tinged pink and his canines had transformed into long, pointy fangs. I leaned back into the sofa, instinctually shying away from him. I trusted him and was comfortable around him but my body reacted nonetheless. His face turned contrite and his fangs seemed to recede into his gums until they looked like normal teeth again. He didn't make a move to get any closer to me. He looked into my eyes with a pained expression and spoke softly.

45

"This is what I am."

I reminded myself that I had only gotten what I asked for. I wanted to see it and he had shown me. It was unfair to make him feel uncomfortable. I urged the tension out of my body and I answered him in a clear voice. "I know. I am sorry for reacting badly. I told you it was okay and it is. I guess, the fangs were a little shocking. I wasn't expecting it."

"Sophie you don't have to apologize. Are you ready to start on our papers?" He said fluidly changing the subject.

Happy to see the awkward moment go, I nodded my agreement and we passed the next hour and a half going back and forth over the project. Lucas definitely didn't need my help but it was fun to swap ideas and debate viewpoints with him. He was incredibly smart and had a great ability to see both sides of an argument.

After we had accomplished a decent amount of work and reached a good stopping point in our assignment, I closed all my books and looked at Lucas. He had never even brought out a book and seemed to be doing his from memory. I was tiny bit envious of his talent but I had enjoyed working with him.

I was stacking my books back up when he asked, "Do you like music?"

"Yea, I love music. I listen to just about anything."

As I answered, he rose from the sofa and walked over to a dark wooden cabinet in the corner of the room, it didn't look like it was from this century but when he opened the doors, I saw an impressive and very modern stereo system inside. He pressed a few buttons and the sound of "21 guns" by Greenday filled the room. I smiled at hearing one of my favorite bands.

"This isn't what I was expecting" I knew my face had given away my surprise.

"What were you expecting?" he asked, chuckling.

"I don't know…classical music or at least something older than me. I just assumed your tastes would run parallel with your age"

He laughed loudly and came to sit next to me on the couch. "You make me sound like someone's grandfather. I'll admit I am a great deal older than you but I adapt with the times and I appreciate a lot of modern things. I do listen to classical music but I also listen to modern music as well as music from all the eras in between."

"Okay, I can admit that I was vampire stereotyping" a giggle slipping out of my mouth.

I looked up, to his face and he met my eyes. His face had taken on a hungry look; I gulped a little and was glad that I trusted him. His face slowly started drawing closer to mine and I tensed. Was he going to kiss me? Did I want him to? Yes and Yes. He was so close that I could feel his cool breath on my cheek. Then his lips met mine and I marveled in the feel of it. It was a wonderful kiss and I was feeling more connected with him than I had felt with anyone before. His lips were firm and definitely below normal temperature but it felt natural. I lifted my hands and ran them through his thick brown hair as his hands ran up my arms and then rested on each side of my face.
His clean and invigorating smell filled my nose and I was lost.
Gradually, he pulled back and stared at me, his grey eyes intense. My breath was shallow and I was having a hard time gathering my thoughts. His lips spread in to a lazy smile as he spoke.

"You make me feel things that I haven't felt since I was human."

I laughed nervously and ran a hand through my hair. How was I supposed to respond to that? My head was spinning; I had just kissed a vampire and enjoyed it! Before I could come up with something reasonable to say to him, my cellphone started ringing. I pulled it out of my pocket to answer. It was my mom asking when I was going to be home. I glanced out the window and realized it had gotten dark. I told her I was on the way and hung up. I looked over at Lucas, he was sitting silently with a half grin on his face. I started to speak and tell him that I had to leave but he spoke first.

"I know you have to go. Vampire hearing, remember?"

I giggled as we both rose from the couch. I gathered my stuff and he walked me to the door. I turned to look at him.

"Thanks for helping me study. I had fun. I guess, I'll see you tomorrow."

He smiled down at me and leaned forward. He pressed a quick kiss to my forehead and said "I look forward to it."

With that, I walked out to my car and made the drive home turning everything over in my mind. Lucas was great and I felt comfortable around him but could I really allow myself to overlook the fact that he was a vampire? In the effort of being honest with myself, I was forced to admit that I already had. His being a vampire hadn't affected any of my feelings for him up until this point and I didn't think it was going to. It all boiled down to a few things.

One- I liked Lucas as a friend and it was turning into something more. Two- He was a vampire and no matter how much my head told me to consider that, it didn't affect my feelings at all. Three- I could spend all my time confused and fighting with myself over it or I could just accept it and learn to roll with it. I decided to roll with it. I was a firm believer in fate and I knew whatever was meant to happen, would happen regardless. When I pulled into my driveway, my head was clear. I was smiling to myself as I walked up the steps to my front porch. Feeling a little floaty and lost in thought, I almost missed something lying on the top stair. I bent to retrieve it. I examined it in the glow from the porch light. It was a deeply colored pink rose and its light scent filled my nose. My mind went from easy to confused. Who was giving me roses? I was still standing on the steps wondering when I got the intense sensation of being watched. Goosebumps broke out on my arms and a chill slithered down my back. I quickly made my way to the door and inside the house. I called out a hello to my mom who was in the kitchen and made my way up to my bedroom. By the time I reached my room, all traces of my earlier unease had vanished and I shook my head and had a giggle over my overreaction. I was still perplexed by the anonymous roses and I decided I was just tired and a little weirded out by the anonymous roses. They had been left in my car and on my doorstep so they had to be from someone who knew me fairly well but I couldn't think of a single person that would send them without telling me. I pushed it all to the back of my mind as I showered and changed into my pajamas and when I went to bed that night I felt safe and reassured.

CHAPTER 5

I walked across the school parking lot with a smile
on my face. I had stayed late to tutor some
freshman and it was dark as I made my way to my
car. I thought back over the past two weeks since
my kiss with Lucas. We hadn't declared ourselves
an official couple or anything but we had hung out a
lot and he had kissed me every time I saw him.
Sometimes it was just a peck and others it was a
heart stopping kiss. We had gone to the movies
and even out to dinner once, I was the only one
that had eaten but it still counted in my book. A few
times I had considered asking him if we were a
couple or not but each time I decided that I
preferred to just wait and see how things panned
out. He had amazed me by how normal he was.
Other than when he drank a glass of blood, it was
easy to forget that he was a vampire. Conversation
with him was fluid and surprisingly modern. We had
discussed everything from books and movies to my
family and my personal goals. Every time I saw him
my heart did a flip flop and I found him as charming
as ever. Everything seemed to be going my way.
The only hitch in my happiness was the roses. I
had gotten a total of twelve with them always
appearing in odd intimate places. I had found the
last one the night before when I opened my window
to let in the breeze. It had been lying on the sill.
That one had shaken me the most. My second
story window wasn't easy to access, so someone
had put a lot of effort into placing it there. I had

mentioned the roses to a few people and I seemed to be the only one who found them alarming. Nora suggested I had a secret admirer and Lucas seemed to think that maybe my mom was behind them. I had asked my mother about it once or twice but not wanting to worry her I didn't bring them back up. I reached my car on the far side of the lot deep in thought. As I reached for the door handle I heard a scuffing sound behind me. A shiver went over me and I was halfway through turning around when I felt a large hairy hand clamp down over my mouth and a huge frame pressed against the back of me as an arm snaked its way around both of mine and clamped down on me like a vice. Terror welled inside of me. My first instinct was to freeze. As my body went rigid my keys fell from my hand and the stranger began dragging me backwards away from my car. I pushed at my fear and tried to think. What could I do? I was still searching for answers when I heard the sound of an idling car. My brain went into over drive. I had no idea who was trying to kidnap me but I was not getting into a car so I could be drug off to only god knows where so they could do as they pleased with me. My body sprang into action and I pushed outward with both of my arms with as much force as I could find, suddenly my arms were free and I started clawing at the beefy hand that was clamped over my mouth. I struggled to go forward and then I was free and falling face down toward the asphalt. I threw my hands out to catch myself and felt skin scraping off my palms as I hit the ground. I scrambled to get up but I felt the stranger's body knock into mine and I was back on the ground with my arms pinned to my side. I went into panic mode and began screaming as I tried to wiggle away, tiny pebbles on the asphalt digging into my arms and a section of my stomach where my t-shirt had ridden up. Abruptly, I was rolled over and my vision was filled with the face of my opponent. He was hideous with scraggly black hair and a matching heavy beard that was covered in flecks of what seemed to be food. His pock marked skin was sprinkled with oozing boils and his beady black eyes were shadowed by a heavy unibrow. He had a mouth filled with yellow teeth framed with blubbery lips. His nose was large and protruded at a sharp angle. I paused in my struggling and a scream died in my throat. He was literally the ugliest man I had ever seen and for the first time, I noticed he smelled awful. It reminded me of sulfur. He was smiling down at me maliciously and he began to open his mouth as if he was going to speak. I closed my eyes and cringed, only imaging how bad his breath could be, I didn't want him speaking so close to my face. Unexpectedly, his weight lifted off of me and his face swam far from my vision as I heard him let out a deep "oomph" as he seemed to hurtle up and away from me. I heard him land with a thud. As I started to sit up and jump to my feet a hand was extended in front of me. I took and pulled myself to my feet shaking my head to clear some of the fuzziness. I looked at my savior and I saw a familiar and handsome face looking at me with a serious

54

expression. I would remember it anywhere. I was looking into the eyes of the vampire who had attacked me on my way home from the coffee shop. I started backing away from him. My mind was a jumbled mess. What was he doing here and why did he seem to be helping me? Who was the man that had tried to kidnap me? None of it made sense. I had stepped back a few feet when I heard a venomous voice from behind me.

"Leave her....She is for my master."

I spun around and saw my attempted kidnapper had gotten to his feet and was staring at the vampire. I was stuck in the middle of them. Great! I thought about running but knowing vampires have amazing speed that didn't seem very logical. Not knowing what else to do I decided to wait and see if they would get distracted enough for me to make it to my car. I turned back to look at the vampire and nearly bumped into his chest. He had crept up behind me and now there were mere centimeters between us. He looked over me to the other man and spoke, his voice as velvet and alluring as I remembered.

"Who is your master and what does this girl mean to him?"

"That is none of your concern. Leave now or I will kill you."

The vampire didn't show any reaction to the death threat. Looking up at him, I felt my insides flutter and I realized that even though he had stolen my blood and left me for dead, I was drawn to him. I looked deep into myself but I couldn't find any fear. I shook my head wondering how that was possible. I should be afraid. The logical part of my mind was screaming at me to be afraid but my feelings didn't respond. Standing so close to him, the feeling of safety started to seep through me. The vampire never looking down at me answered the man, his voice carrying a confidence that it must have taken many years to gain.

"I was hoping you would say that."

Then he leapt over me and tackled the man. It was so quick, that my mind was still registering it as I spun around to look at the two. They were struggling on the ground rolling one another over, each with his hands at the other's throat. The vampire's fangs were out and the man seemed to have turned a sickly gray. I was stuck wondering what to do. I wanted to run to my car and speed away as fast as possible but for some reason I couldn't take my eyes off the vampire. As I watched, the vampire managed to struggle to his feet dragging the other man with him. He had his arms locked around the other's throat and he leaned in as if he was going to bite him. That was when I saw my would be abductor snake a hand into his tattered coat pocket and bring out a wooden stake. He lifted his arm, swinging it toward the vampire. I couldn't let the vampire die. I didn't know why I wanted to save him but I did. I threw my hands in front of me and ran forward screaming "STOP!" before I could reach for the man, I felt my hands grow warm and was blinded by light as orange and yellow fire shot from my hands like a laser beam and hit the man in the chest. He caught fire quickly and as if he was kindling, was immediately engulfed. He started to scream and threw himself to the ground thrashing as the vampire, apparently unharmed, quickly backed away. I stood in shock with my hands still out fire still streaming from them and landing on the already burning man. How did I do that? It should be impossible but the last few weeks had taught me that anything was possible. Gradually, the fire ebbed and then stopped altogether. I brought my hands up in front of my face to inspect them. There wasn't a single mark on them; it was like the fire had never happened. I flipped them over and continued examining them in awe until the vampire approached me and placed his cool hands over mine, lowering them down from my face. I looked up into his face and his expression was unreadable. A moment before everything had seemed so far away but it all came rushing to the surface. I tried to wrap my mind around it all. I had almost been kidnapped and then saved by a vampire who had tried to kill me then fire had shot out from my hands to save him. Looking into the vampire's eyes, everything calmed inside me and I realized I couldn't hear the screams of the man I had set on fire anymore. My eyes started to scan the parking lot, wondering if he had gotten away. I noticed a large puddle of black liquid, little wisps of smoke rising from it. It had to be what was left of the man. I started toward it to verify my assumption but a firm grip on my arm stopped me. Again, I turned to face the vampire. His perfect features remained calm and his voice was low when he spoke.

"You didn't know you could do that?"

I tried to answer but my throat felt like it had swollen shut so I just stood opening and closing my mouth without making a sound like a fish out of water. He didn't say anything and his expression didn't change. He just stood waiting. Finally, my answer came croaking through my lips

"No. Who are you?
He placed his hands in the pockets of his dark wash jeans, his gaze sweeping over my face.
"My name is Daire and as you've guessed I am a vampire."

Well that was direct. A million questions flowed through my mind and I hurled the first one.

"Why did you save me?"

His mouth quirked up at the corner.

"You are too interesting to lose.....for now."

A chill ran over me and I wanted to be afraid but I still couldn't muster up any fear.

"That doesn't make any sense. You tried to kill me before."

"That was a mistake on my part. I didn't know then what I know now."

Wow...cryptic much? Everything still wasn't making sense to me so I continued my questioning.

"Before you knew me? You've only seen me twice!"

His eyebrow lifted as if in question.

"No. You've only seen me twice. I have seen you much more than that. Do you like roses, Blondie?"

I had a dawning moment and I realized what he meant.

"The roses. You left them. You were watching me."

"Yes."

"Why?"

"Call it curiosity. You resisted enthrallment. I have been alive a long time and I have met only a handful of people with that ability and I have never met a human with the ability. After tonight, I have my answer."

"Your answer?"

"You're a witch."

"WHAT? I think I'd know if I was a witch."

My words came out in a rush with a slightly hysterical tone. A witch? There was no way.

"Yes, witches are the only beings I have met that can conjure and manipulate fire at will. However, you are peculiar in the simple fact that you didn't know. Most witches come of age and can use their power around the age of twelve. Yours seem to have just manifested."

Everything seemed to be spinning and my chest started burning. Without thought, I sat down right where I was standing. I leaned forward and put my head between my knees, locking my arms around them. This couldn't be happening! It was one thing to accept that there were things in the world that humans had no idea of but it was something else entirely to think that I was one of those things. Everything he said made sense. I mean, I had never heard of a normal human shooting fire from their hands, so there had to be truth in his words. Was my life a lie? Did I get it from my parents? Was my mom a witch? Was I defective since I got my powers late? Did I even have them now? I hadn't meant to shoot fire from my hands, it just happened. Maybe, I couldn't do anything else. It was all too much and I started to do something I absolutely hated. I started to cry. Hot tears ran down my face and dripped to the ground. Once I started, it was like I couldn't stop. Silent tears turned into racking sobs that echoed across the empty parking lot. I kept my face toward the ground until the tears ebbed and I was left feeling hollow. I finally lifted my head and realized Daire was still standing there looking at me with a curious expression. I had forgotten that I had an audience and I tucked my hair behind my ear nervously. His eyes were intense as if I was a puzzle he couldn't quite figure out. Hesitantly he extended his hand toward me and for the second time that night, pulled me to my feet. I dusted off my backside somewhat self-consciously. A question flashed across my mind.

"What was that guy?" I motioned toward the still smoking puddle.

Daire's eyebrows lifted a little.

"My, my, you are perceptive. He was a goblin. They can enchant themselves to appear human but the boils give them away and it's hard for them to maintain it under stress. You may have noticed him turning gray. That was the enchantment wearing off. They are very hard to kill. Fortunately, you chose one of their weaknesses. Fire."

Vampires, witches and goblins? I didn't think it was possible for me to ever be shocked again.

"Chose? I didn't choose anything. It just happened." I noticed that some anger had seeped into my voice and I tried to tone it down. I wasn't afraid but I couldn't imagine yelling at vampire to be a good idea.

"Witches guard their secrets heavily, especially against other supernatural beings so I can't tell you exactly how your powers work but I do know that your will is what caused it. Trained witches will something to happen and it does. You wanted to hurt him and you did. It's a simple as that."

He made me sound so callous. I didn't want to kill the goblin, it was an accident. With that thought, something else manifested itself in my mind. I wasn't sure if I wanted to know the answer but I had to ask

"Are goblins nice? I know that one was trying to kidnap me but did he have a family and friends? Did he have a normal life somewhere?"

Daire rolled his eyes, obviously unimpressed by my attempt at compassion.

"No. Goblins are notorious loners. They reproduce but there is no family aspect involved. They are nasty little beings and have no regard for humans. Actually, they eat them."

Oddly, I was unfazed by his proclamation and I felt a little better. I had been feeling guilty about being a murderer, accident or not but I'd choose that over being eaten any day.

"So he was going to eat me? What is the deal? First you and now him!" Frustration was evident in my voice.

Daire's mouth lifted a fraction in amusement.

"It is unfortunate, isn't it? However, I don't think he intended to eat you. He said you were for his master."

"Master?"

"Yes. Goblins are frequently employed by more powerful beings. Vampires, demons and that sort. In exchange for their servitude they are given protection from others."

Great, now there were demons. You learn about one paranormal creature and it's all downhill from there.

"Who is his master and what does he want from me?"

"That's a million dollar question, isn't it?"

"Does that mean you don't know or that you aren't telling me?"

"I don't know but I am going to find out."

"Why?"

"I believe there is an old proverb about gift horses and mouths. Call it curiosity."

"So you're saying it's a gift? Is that a type of apology for trying to kill me?"

He stepped closer to me, so that there was a hair width between us. He bored his blue eyes into mine and yet, I still wasn't afraid. Instead, a tingle went through me in acknowledgment that his body was so close to mine that I could smell him. It was intoxicating and reminded me of a cross between cedar and sandalwood. I scanned his face, taking in its perfection. He was beautiful. I had never used that word to describe a man before but that's what he was. He spoke, his voice rich but unfeeling.

"Blondie, I don't apologize. Especially, not for trying to kill someone. I am a vampire. Humans mean nothing to me. As I said, call it curiosity."

I knew it was cheeky but wanting to show that I wasn't afraid I said "Since you like proverbs so much, haven't you heard that curiosity killed the cat?"

There was no mistaking the sarcasm in my voice but he seemed unfazed as he answered.

"Then it's fortunate I'm not a cat then."

I stood with no answer my head tilted toward the ground. I had run out of questions and a bone deep weariness had seeped into me. I just wanted to go home and sleep.

He leaned down toward my ear and I stepped back a few inches as his hand came to rest under my chin. He tilted my head up and gave me an amused look.

"It's wise to be afraid of me."

I looked at him unflinching as I answered.

65

"I'm not afraid, I'm just not stupid. I haven't forgotten the last time I let you near my neck. As a matter of fact, the scar will always be there."

I was too tired to keep the weariness out of my voice and his amusement seemed to fade at my words. He leaned forward until his lips were inches from mine and it took all my resolve not to back away. As tired as I was, I refused to be intimidated. When he spoke I could feel his cool breath flutter across my lips and the urge to lean away left me.

"Go home."

With that simple statement he straightened and turned away. I put my hand on his arm and he paused.

"What about the Goblin and his car? Isn't someone going to notice that?" I gestured toward the puddle and the old car I now noticed was sitting a few spots away, still idling.

He turned back to face me and let out a sigh with a slight roll of his eyes. Then he snapped his fingers and I saw the puddle and car disappear. They were there one minute and then "Poof!" They were gone. Then he held his hand out and my keys flew from the ground a few feet away to float through the air and land gently in his upturned palm. He lifted my hand from my side and dropped them into it. I couldn't stop myself from asking as my eyes grew wide.

"How did you do that?"

"Go home."

I had questions but I was only too happy to agree. He was obviously tired of my company and even though I wasn't afraid, I was too tired to deal with an angry vampire. I turned toward my car.

"One more thing Blondie, I wouldn't mention me to Lucas. You would hate for him to die."

I spun around ready to confront him. I had completely forgotten about Lucas but now he was the forefront of my thoughts and I was angry to have him threatened but Daire was gone, like he had disappeared into thin air.

I walked to my car only a little shaky. The night seemed like a dream. I replayed everything in my head as I drove home and I still had so many questions. When I reached my house I walked in and immediately realized that my mom and Bailey were in bed. I had told her I would be staying late after school so she wouldn't wait up for me but I knew she was listening for me to come in. It was a relief not to have to face her. She could always pick up on when something was wrong with me and there was no way I was going to try to explain my night to her. When I reached my bedroom, I knew my first order of business was a shower. Grabbing a pair of cheerleading shorts a tank top and under garments I retreated into my bathroom. I turned on the water and as I waited for it to heat up I peeled my clothes off, grimacing when I realized my shirt was ruined. It had tiny holes all over it and it was covered in dirt. I dropped my clothes into the hamper and got to work disinfecting all the minor cuts and scrapes I had gained. Done with that, I stepped into the steaming shower and tried to think of anything other than what I had just been through. It didn't work. After my shower, I dressed and brushed my teeth while I tried to compartmentalize everything that had happened. I decided that my first concern was Lucas. What did Daire mean? He had threatened to kill Lucas and I had no doubt that he would make good on it. I for sure wasn't going to test the theory no matter how much I wanted Lucas's opinion. Turning Daire's words over in my mind, I realized that he had told me not to tell Lucas about him. He hadn't said I couldn't tell him about everything else. I finished brushing my teeth and walked from the bathroom to my bedroom. I found my cellphone and dialed Lucas. After three rings, I heard his voice on the other end and it was a welcome sound.

"Hello."

"Hey, it's Sophie." My voice was small and weak.

"Are you alright? You sound upset."

"Yea I'm okay but do you think you could meet me at the reserve tomorrow? I have some things I wanted to talk to you about."

"Sure, as long as you're okay. What time?"

"Well tomorrow is Saturday so do you think you could meet me at one o'clock?"

"I'll be there."

"Thanks. See you then."

"I look forward to it."

I heard the click in my ear signaling that he had hung up. I closed my phone and laid back on the bed. I was confused about a lot of things but knowing that I could talk to Lucas about it made things seem much easier to handle. I just knew he would help me figure all this out. The only thing I knew he wouldn't be able to help me with was Daire. I was shocked at myself for having not been afraid of him but even more so I was curious about him. Who was he and why did he help me? I couldn't bring myself to think that he went around saving people often and he had been so cryptic about everything that I just didn't know what to make of him. Later, laying in the dark, I thought I would never get to sleep. I was bone tired but I couldn't get my mind to shut off. However, I gradually managed to drift into sleep with Daire's face hovering in my mind.

CHAPTER 6

I woke the next day stiff and groggy. The night
came rushing back. I looked at the clock on my
nightstand and realized it was noon. I had slept
later than I normally did. I jumped out of bed and
winced a little at the soreness in my muscles. After
brushing my teeth, I rushed through dressing,
deciding on jean shorts, flip-flops and a simple pink
tank top. I threw my hair into a pony tail and
headed to the kitchen for breakfast. There was a
note on the fridge from my mom telling me that she
and Bailey were visiting a family friend and would
be back later. Since, I still wasn't sure I could see
her without alerting her to something being wrong, I
was thankful. After a bowl of oatmeal and some
coffee, I was out the door and headed to the
reserve.

When I pulled into the parking Lot of the
reserve, I noticed Lucas's car already in a spot and
he was standing outside propped against the
driver's door. I had no idea how I was going to have
this conversation with him but I couldn't help but
smile. Seeing him made me feel like everything
would be okay. In that moment I realized that in
only a few weeks I had come to depend on his
friendship. I wasn't sure that I was glad to know
about all the things that went bump in the night but I
was glad I had Lucas in my life and that never
would have happened without knowing. That
thought made it all easier to handle. I pulled up
beside his car and hopped out. I walked to the front

of the car and he met me there, smiling. He held out his hand and I placed mine in his. We were headed toward the trail when he spoke.

"So what did you want to talk about?"

"Last night I was attacked." I began with my voice only a little shaky. He gave me a surprised look but said nothing. "I'll give you the short version. I left after tutoring and in the parking lot a man grabbed me and tried drag me away. We struggled and when I got free....." I paused and looked over at him. He was looking at me with an encouraging expression so I continued. "...and then fire shot out of my hands and he went up in flames. He burned and ended up a puddle of black nastiness."

I had managed to leave Daire out of the conversation completely. Whew! It troubled me some to lie to him but knowing that I was keeping him from Daire lessened my guilt. I waited for his response. I couldn't guess his reaction but I knew that he would believe me. His voice was informative when he spoke.

"Sounds like you're a witch and were attacked by a goblin."

I thought it was a little odd that he wasn't surprised but chalked it up to the fact that he was a vampire and probably hadn't been surprised in quite a few

72

decades. He looked at me and I knew he was gauging my reaction. Having heard this news before but not wanting to explain that to Lucas, I opted for interested.

"A witch? Goblin?"

Unexpectedly, a look of relief flashed over his face so quickly that I almost missed it and then his expression went calm as he answered.

"Yea, they are the only beings I know of that can create and manipulate fire. It's deadly to most other super naturals and most of them fear it. Even a vampire can die from fire if they burn long enough. Most witches gain their powers early in life but unless you had these before you are unique, getting yours late. As far as goblins go, they are evil buggers that usually work for another supernatural."

When he stopped, I was relieved. Now, I could get some answers.

"If I am a witch does that mean that one of my parents was?"

"No. Sometimes, power can lay dormant in a bloodline for many generations. It just means that one of your ancestors was. Generally the secret is handed down along with a few talismans until it reaches the next person with power but if your parents haven't mentioned it then it is probable that the secret was lost in your family. That also answers the question of why you resisted enthrallment. Witches are immune."

"Well, what do I do now?"

"Honestly? I'm not really sure. My knowledge of witches is limited."

"Don't I have to learn to use my powers or whatever? Don't I need a teacher or something?"

"No. As far as I know, when witches gain their magic they know how to use it. It just happens. As a vampire I have a few powers but nothing like a witch's, so I have no idea how to help you learn yours."

I felt a little dejected. I was supposed to know how to use my powers but I didn't. Not only was I a freak, I was a broken one.

"Okay. Well, what do you think I should do?"

"Just give it time. Maybe it comes in stages. I am alarmed that you were attacked, though. Did the Goblin say anything to you?"

"Umm…something about his master wanting me but that was it."

"I don't like the implication that has. I'm not sure why but someone believed you were valuable enough to have kidnapped and that makes me nervous. Please be careful from now on. Try not to go anywhere alone and please try to avoid being out after dark. I am going to do some digging and see if I can come up with some answers."

He was telling me not to be alone? I'm not a hermit but I like my free time, so the idea didn't sit well with me. Not wanting to worry him or argue I nodded my agreement. We had made the full circle of the trail and were back to the parking lot. We walked to my car in silence and when we reached it he let go of my hand that he had been holding since the beginning. He opened my door for me and leaned down to press a kiss to my forehead. Not wanting my time with him to end so quickly I spoke.

"Do you want to go catch a movie or something?"

"I would but I want to head and do some research on all this. The faster I have some answers the faster I can stop worrying about you."

He answered with a smile. I felt a little put out that he didn't invite me along but since we hadn't declared ourselves a couple I reminded myself that I had no right to be clingy.

"Okay. I guess, I'll see you later."

"Yes. Please be careful and remember what I said. I can't stand the idea of anything happening to you."

I smiled when his words sent a warm feeling through me. He pressed another kiss to my head and walked away.

Later that afternoon, I was sitting in my room still thinking everything over. Honestly, how could I think about anything else? Lucas had told me to wait and see what happened but I was supposed to be a witch and I felt defective for not knowing what to do. A tiny spark of idea started in my mind and then grew until I had to carry it out. My mom and Bailey hadn't made it home yet and I had the house to myself. I made my way out of the house into the back yard. It was surrounded by trees and I knew no one would be able to see me since there weren't many houses nearby and our property extended well into the surrounding trees. I stood in the middle of the back yard and stood with my hands thrust out in front of me. I concentrated as hard as I could. I willed fire to come from my hands. I had my eyes squeezed shut and after a moment everything seemed to fade away. I couldn't hear the birds anymore. I couldn't hear anything but the sound of my heart beat. I concentrated harder. I was determined to do this. Finally, I felt a warmth spread from my chest and flow down my arms to rest in my hands. Cautiously, I cracked on eye open. There in my palm was a ball of flame. It didn't stream out the way it had the night before but instead sat flickering calmly. My mouth dropped open. I had done it! A laugh escaped me and I wondered if I could toss the fire away from me the way I had before. As soon as the thought popped into my mind, the flame shot from my hand streaming out to land on the ground. It snaked through the grass setting in ablaze. I laughed loudly, pleased with myself. It seemed that once I started, it got easier. Feeling daring, I concentrated and the flames crawled and looped on itself until my name was written in fire on the back lawn. It was in cursive print and each letter was as tall as me. A grin split my face. Maybe, being a witch wasn't so bad after all. I could feel energy flowing freely throughout my body and it was like nothing I had felt before. I was so energized! I felt like I could run forever and never get tired. After a few giggly moments, I decided I should probably stop. I wanted the fire to go out and it did. In the blink of an eye it had flickered out. I breathed out in relief. I hadn't thought that far ahead and I would have been in trouble if I couldn't make it go out. With a glance at the grass, I realized I was still in trouble. My name was burned into the lawn, the grass black and crispy where the flames had been. What was I going to do? There was no way I could explain it to my mom, and she would freak when she saw it. Thinking quick, I closed my eyes and concentrated I felt the energy flare inside of me and I opened my eyes. The wind picked up and all the black grass

77

started to flake and blow away. I watched until it was all gone leaving nothing but raw dirt. Not good enough. Now my name was there in dirt instead of burnt grass. I focused and thought harder. Before my eyes, new grass started bursting through the dirt. Green blades shot up impossibly fast and a moment later all the dirt was covered and the lawn looked exactly the way it had before my little experiment. Exhilarated and feeling confident, I tried something new. I focused hard and heavy raindrops began to fall. Looking around me, I realized it was only falling in a large circle of the back yard. I willed it to stop and it did. It was amazing. I couldn't believe that I was doing this! That morning I was thinking that I had drawn the ancestral short straw but being able to make something happen just because I wanted it to it was something I had never even dreamed of. Not knowing when my mom would be back, I decided it was best to head inside. Once in my room, I continued my experimenting with small things like having my cellphone float across the room to land in my palm. By that evening, I was exhausted. Apparently, magic takes a lot out of you. I was even more tired than I had been the night before. I crawled into bed early that night, a little worried over what Lucas might find out about my attempted kidnapping but mostly awed by the magic I had discovered.

CHAPTER 7

A week after discovering that I was a witch, I was sitting at The Drip, sipping a vanilla latte and reading a trashy romance novel. They were one of my secret addictions. It was typical with a bare chested, long haired hunk on the front. I was immersed in a love scene when I heard the legs of the chair across the table from me scrape across the floor. I brought the book down from in front of my face, smiling. When I saw the man in the chair across from me, my face fell. It wasn't who I was expecting.

"Daire? What are you doing here?"

"You drink that stuff?" he motioned toward my coffee.

"Yes."

"It smells putrid." He lips curved downward in disgust.

"Okay, now that you have insulted my beverage habits, I'll ask you again. What are you doing here?"

"Now, now Blondie don't be rude. Aren't you the least bit curious to know if I found anything out about your little goblin incident?"

I scoffed. I hadn't seen him since that night and I had forgotten that he had said he was going to look into it. Lucas had been so reassuring when he said that he would look into it that I hadn't been worried about getting answers from Daire. He was a mystery to me still and the fact that I wasn't afraid of him bothered me. I should be afraid and I was always peeved when I ignored my common sense. I had done my best over the week to push him from my mind entirely but it seemed like the harder I pushed it away, the more his face appeared. I could recall it in vivid detail and when I thought of how close we had stood that night my stomach churned. Being honest with myself, I could admit that I was attracted to him in a way that I hadn't known was possible. I could also admit that it wasn't a good thing. I had Lucas and I liked him, the last thing I needed was to have feelings for a homicidal vampire. That would be classified as an unhealthy relationship to say the least. Determined not to feel anything toward him but annoyance I glared at him from across the table. I could feel my stomach start to churn and I knew I had failed. Giving up, I let out a sigh.

"Actually, I have Lucas looking into it for me. Oh by the way, He'll be here in a few minutes and given your apparent feelings on him, I think it's best if you leave."

"Why do you care about him?"

Angry that he was bringing my feelings for Lucas into question, my voice was filled with venom when I answered him.

"He has been nice to me since we met. He offered answers when I woke up confused after you left me for dead; answers that I know were hard for him to give me. He bared his past for me so that I would understand. We are friends. What do you have against him anyways?"

He sat reclined in the chair, his arms crossed in front of him with his sapphire eyes staring into mine. His face was puzzled as if I had said something he didn't understand and he was trying to see the answer inside my head. After a tense moment, he responded.

"You make me sound like a monster yet you glorify him. It could just as easily have been him to attack you."

Had I hurt his feelings? I shook the thought away. If he was that feeling, he wouldn't kill people.

"Lucas doesn't feed on people! He drinks blood from a bag. He behaves with a conscience, while you embrace you inner monster or whatever you want to call it. That's why I glorify him!"

I glanced around at the other patrons, hoping no one had heard my outburst. When none of them so much as looked my way I looked back to Daire. The puzzled look had returned to his face. He spoke his voice low and confident.

"You surprise me, Blondie."

He gave a slight shake of his head as if in disbelief.

"What is that supposed to mean?"

"You'll find out …in time."

"What kind of game are you playing?"

My tone gave away my annoyance and he responded with an icy calm.

"I don't play games."

"You're lying! This whole thing is a game to you! First, you try to kill me then you save me and now you're here questioning my feelings for Lucas. What is the point?"

He leaned forward in chair and looked at me with an intense expression. I could almost see the anger coming off of him in waves. I gulped a little. My mind had been telling me to be afraid and I finally was. I froze under his gaze. His voice vibrated when he spoke, proving his anger.

"I don't lie. I have no need. If I don't want you to know then I won't tell you. It is that simple."

He leaned back in his chair and some of the hardness left his face. Like someone threw a switch, my fear was gone. Not sure where to go with the conversation, I reverted to a previous question.

"What do you have against Lucas?"

He shrugged.

"He tried to kill me."

What?! My first instinct was to tell him that he was lying but his reaction after the last time stopped me. I thought about the possibilities of Lucas trying to kill someone. He had told me he had a dark period and that he had killed people before. Maybe that was when it happened or maybe it was self-defense.

"Why?"

"That's not important at the moment."

Hearing the resolve in his voice, I knew I wasn't going to get a real answer. Instead I decided to question him on something that had been nagging me all week.

"How old are you?"

83

His face didn't change.

"One hundred and ninety nine."

Wow. He was older than Lucas by almost a decade. It meant he was turned into a vampire in 1812. America was still a new country then and I wondered if he was from somewhere else, even though he had no accent.

"Where are you from? How did you turn into a vampire?"

I was wondering if he was going to answer me when he spoke.

"I was born in London in 1790. In the summer of 1812 I was twenty two years old. I went to a ball being thrown by a prestigious couple. There I met a beautiful woman named Charlotte. We danced and I was quite taken with her. We left in my carriage where she enthralled me and turned me. I woke up in an inn a few days later. She explained what had happened and we spent the next few years traveling while she taught me how to be a vampire. Eventually, we parted and over the years I ended up here."

Throughout his story his voice never betrayed any emotion. His face and voice were like stone. I felt awkward sitting there. What do you say to someone who was turned into a monster without their permission? I tried to remember how little human life meant to him but in that moment I felt sorry for him. I almost told him that I was but I didn't think it would have a positive effect. I decided to change the subject.

"I found out that I can do more than make fire."

"It looks like the little witch has found her power."

Suddenly, Daire was on his feet. Looking up and over I realized he was standing nose to nose with Lucas. They were both giving each other murderous looks and I noticed their fangs had extended slightly. I looked around The Drip again, hoping no one was paying attention. They weren't. I was afraid that if I spoke it would set one of them off, so I sat quietly waiting with my heart pounding in my chest and wondering if it was going to end badly. Daire had said he would kill Lucas and I was hoping the public venue would make him reconsider. I decided that if a fight broke out I would try to use my powers to intervene. After a few seconds that were so tense you could pluck them like a string, Lucas backed away a fraction. Daire moved back as well. They separated until there was roughly 3 feet between them. I noticed that Lucas had gravitated toward me. He reached a hand out and placed it on mine that was lying on

the table. He was clearly making the statement
"She is mine!" Lucas spoke, his teeth clenched.

"Stay away from her."

Daire stood tense and ready, as he replied.

"Why? Maybe you should think about who
you are trying to command."

"Maybe you should do the same."

Daire glanced over at me and then without a word,
turned and walked out of The Drip. As soon as
Daire had made it out of the doors, Lucas looked
down at me. He ran a finger over my cheek and
then went to sit across from me. His voice was
calm when he questioned me.

"How did you meet him?"

It was time to confess. I wasn't sure how Lucas was
going to take the news that I lied to him but I had to
tell him the truth. He had seen Daire so my reason
for lying was gone. I took a deep breath and began.
I explained everything. I told him that it was Daire
who had attacked me and then how he had saved
me a week before. When I was done I stopped and
waited for his reaction. He breathed out a deep sigh
and his gray eyes were pleading when he spoke.

"Sophie, I understand why you lied but you can't do that ever again. I'm a vampire; I can take care of myself. It's flattering that you wanted to protect me but you put yourself in danger. I can't find the answers to this puzzle if you don't give me all the pieces. As for Daire, try to stay away from him. If you see him, call me. He is dangerous and you shouldn't trust him. If he saved you it's because he is trying to use you for something. Don't let him fool you; he is incapable of human emotion."

Well, that was certainly to the point. I pondered his words. I knew it was wrong that I had lied to him and I didn't want to have to do it ever again. Lucas made me happy. I was attracted to him and he was caring and honest. I didn't want to mess it up. We weren't an official couple but I hoped that eventually we would be. Then there was Daire. I knew Lucas absolutely believed what he said about Daire but what if he was wrong? I admitted that I hadn't seen a lot of sincere emotion come from Daire but just minutes before I had seen him get angry. If he was capable of anger wouldn't he be capable of positive emotions too? I didn't believe that someone who had that much inner fire could be emotionless. Some of Lucas's words had sense. I didn't think it was a good idea to be around Daire. I wasn't convinced he was heartless and I wasn't afraid of him but I felt an attraction for him. It was a primal attraction that sat deep in my soul and it scared me. I didn't want to associate with a killer, whether he had feelings or not. Slowly, I nodded my assent to Lucas. His lips curved into his familiar grin and I knew that we were going to be okay. He must have had the same thought because he changed the subject.

"Have you found any new magic?"

"Yea, a little. Nothing like last Saturday though. I learned the hard way that magic takes A LOT out of you. I have just been practicing the small stuff, like floating pens and turning door knobs with my mind."

I had called him last Sunday to let him know about the powers I had discovered. He seemed to be genuinely happy for me and it was nice to have someone who would listen. Ordinarily, I would tell Nora but learning about the paranormal had been a rough experience for me and I didn't want to shove that on her. Lucas was the only person close to me who knew my secret and talking to him was refreshing. He slid his hand across the table and rested it on mine. My heart beat picked up and my breathing got shorter. Would I ever not react like this? Where Daire sent a lightning fast rush through me, Lucas gave me a warm and safe feeling. His gray eyes met mine and he spoke.

"I still haven't found any answers to why you were attacked and I've looked into your background to try to find were your powers come from but I haven't had any luck."

I had asked him if he had found anything every day that week. His answer had been the same every time. It was a little disheartening. When he had called me earlier and asked me to meet him at The Drip, I had assumed that he had found something. Unable to disguise my disappointment, I answered.

"Oh...okay. Thanks for still looking. If you didn't have any information for me, why did you ask me to meet you here?"

He smiled at me and I felt his cool hand give mine a little squeeze as he answered.

"I just wanted to see you. You're the best part of my day."

I felt the smile split my face. It was going to be a good day after all.

CHAPTER 8

"A girl can never have too many shoes!"

Nora spoke as we walked across the parking lot. Yesterday, I had spent a few enjoyable hours at The Drip talking to Lucas and today Nora and I had spent the day on retail therapy. I was feeling more carefree than I had in weeks. Yesterday's run in with Daire was far from my mind and I felt like a normal teenager again. It had gotten dark a little while before and the stores in the shopping center were beginning to close. I smiled at Nora's comment.

"Agreed. You ready to head home? The stores are starting to close and I think we've done enough damage to our wallets for today."

"Yea, my mom is going to kill me if she realizes I bought so much."

I let out a giggle as we got close to my car. I was pulling my keys from my pocket when I felt the wave of energy. I looked over at Nora and realized she had felt it too. She was looking at me with a strange expression on her face and then she slowly started to rise off the ground. I dropped my shopping bags and tried to reach out for her but I realized that I had started to rise off the ground too. The energy surrounded me and it was so thick it was almost touchable. I tried to look around but I realized I was stuck. I couldn't move. Remembering my own power I focused and tried to push the foreign energy away but it didn't so much as waver. Nora had panic in her eyes and wasn't moving so I deduced that she was stuck too. I tried to speak to her, calm her but my mouth was locked shut. We had stopped rising and were hovering about a foot off the ground. I heard footsteps and saw a man step out from behind a nearby parked car. He was tall and handsome but his face held no emotion. His face was stone as he walked toward us. He was wearing a gray suit complete with a tie and dress shoes. He walked with determination and I knew he was evil. Fear welled up inside me and if I hadn't been frozen I would have run. I was terrified just by looking at him. His shoulder length blonde hair was angelic and it framed a face that had strong features. It was his eyes that gave away his nature. They were black and soulless, like empty caverns. They reminded me of a doll. They looked like eyes but it was apparent that there was no life behind them. I pushed against the energy as hard as I could, desperate to get away. I knew this man meant me harm. I was still frozen when he came to stand before me. I was a foot off the ground and he was still eye level with me. I stopped struggling and waited to see if he would speak. When he did, his voice surrounded me like icy water, sending chills down my spine and goose bumps over my arms.

"So, you're Sophie? It's amazing how one so young and naïve can be so important. I see the fear in your eyes, don't worry I have no plans to harm you, yet. I also see the confusion. Who I am and why I am here is irrelevant."

He stepped forward to me and drew a small dagger out of his pocket along with a vial. At the sight of the knife I started to struggle again but it was still useless. He reached out and pulled my wrist to him. Quickly, he swiped the blade down my forearm. The pain of it seared through me but frozen, I couldn't react. Blood immediately welled up in the wound and poured over the sides of my arm, spilling onto the ground. Never even looking up at me, he angled my arm down so the blood ran over my hand and off of my fingertips. He placed the vial underneath it and it was quickly filled with blood. I felt nauseous at the sight of all my blood spilling out. He released my arm but it was frozen were he had left it and despite my efforts I couldn't move it. He capped the vial and returned it and the knife to his pocket. He stepped back a foot and returned his gaze to me. He snapped his fingers and the wound in my arm was gone. There wasn't even any evidence of the blood that had run over my skin. He had healed me? Why? His voice broke me from my questions.

"Until we meet again, Sophie...."

With a snap of his fingers, he was gone. Nora and I hovered for a split second longer and then dropped to the ground. The unexpected drop caused us both to buckle at the knees and fall forward onto the pavement. We scrambled to our feet and I turned to Nora. Her face was shocked and her mouth was opening and closing furiously. It was the first time I had ever seen her speechless. I rushed forward and threw my arms around her. I had no idea why the man had taken my blood but I knew I couldn't live without Nora. I was so relieved that she was safe. She returned my hug tightly until I heard her choked words.

"What the hell was that about and how did he do that?"

"I don't know."

"You don't know? I don't believe you Sophie Ann and you better explain right now. Are you in some kind of trouble? I repeat how did he do that?"

I debated a second and decided that it was time for another confession. I hated lying to her anyways.

"I can explain some of it but I really don't know who that was or what he wanted with me. Can we get in the car? I need to call Lucas. Just give me a few minutes and I'll explain everything I can."

"If Lucas has gotten you mixed up in something, I'll strangle him! You promise to explain?"

"It wasn't Lucas and Yes."

"Okay."

We gathered our bags and climbed into my car. I found my cell phone that I had left lying in between the seats and dialed Lucas. He picked up after the first ring.

"Hello Beautiful."

"I need to come see you. Are you at home?"

"Yes. What's wrong?"

"I'll explain when I get there. I am bringing Nora too. Something happened and we have to give her some answers."

"Okay.....are you sure?"

"Positive. I'll see you in a minute."

I hung up the phone and headed toward Lucas's house. Nora sat silently in the passenger seat the whole way. When she looked over at me I tried to give her a reassuring smile but she just went back to staring out the window. I spent the entire 15 minute drive praying that I wouldn't lose my best friend.

We pulled up in front of Lucas's house and he was waiting on the porch. I climber out and walked to him quickly, Nora close behind.

94

Wordlessly he motioned toward the opened door and we all walked in and made our way to the twin sofas in his living room. Nora and I sat on one and Lucas sat opposite of us. Nora was still silent as I gave Lucas a rundown of what had happened. When I finished I looked to Nora but continued speaking to him.

"We have to tell her."

My eyes were still on Nora when he answered.

"I could enthrall her so she would forget."

I saw Nora's eyes grow wide as I turned to him.

"NO! She is my best friend, I would never do that to her. I am tired of lying to her and she deserves the truth!"

I was shocked that he had offered that as a solution. I turned back to Nora who had a normal but slightly puzzled expression.

"Okay…I'll help you explain."

Still looking at Nora, I began.

"You know how I was attacked on the way home from the drip? Well it wasn't an animal." I paused for her reaction and when she nodded I continued "It was a man. I know this sounds crazy but it was a vampire."

I tensed for her response and to my surprise she burst out laughing.

"Wow, Sophie. That's the best you could do? Did you set this all up? You had me going for a while!"

When I didn't laugh and she saw the serious expression on my face, her amused expression turned to concern.

"You're serious aren't you? Sophie, vampires are myths. You sound like a crazy person."

Not knowing what else to do I looked at Lucas. Taking my signal, he leaned forward and extended his fangs. Nora followed my gaze and when she saw Lucas she jumped up from the couch and started to back away. Lucas retracted his fangs as I got up and grabbed Nora. She was looking at me with fear in her eyes.

"How…How…did he do that?"

"He is a vampire too but he isn't who attacked me."

Nora was freaked but I could tell she wasn't totally convinced.

"Lucas won't hurt you. Don't be afraid. I know it's all so hard to believe. If you'll sit down with me we'll prove everything but don't be afraid. You know I would never let anything happen to you."

I could see my message slowly sink and she went back to sit on the couch. I looked at Lucas again and in the blink of an eye he was across the room. I could see Nora trying to rationalize it in her head and finally when she failed, she looked at me.

"You're telling the truth aren't you?"

"Yes."

Then Nora did the unexpected. She laughed and threw her arms around me.

"This is AWESOME! Who knew? How did you find all this out? I can't believe you have been holding out on me!!! Is there more?"

Lucas and I looked at each other in shock. Nora's reaction wasn't even close to what I had anticipated. I should have known better. Soon I was laughing too and even Lucas had a chuckle. When the giggles subsided Lucas and I explained everything to her. I started at the beginning and told it until the end. I even told her about Daire, although from Lucas's expression he wasn't pleased. Then Nora and I had to fill Lucas in on the events from earlier in the evening. When we finished, her enthusiasm hadn't dimmed.

"Gosh Sophie, This is all so surreal. I mean, I get that it's serious and all but MY BEST FRIEND IS A WITCH!!!"

I laughed. It was typical Nora to find the silver lining and ignore everything else. I checked the time on my cellphone and realized it was almost curfew for Nora and mine wasn't far behind. We headed to the door with Lucas trailing behind us, Nora chattering the whole way. When we made it to the porch I turned to Lucas and Nora gave me a wink said goodbye and headed to the car to wait for me. Lucas and I stood face to face and he spoke.

"Well, I think Nora took it well."

"Yea, that's Nora."

He had a smile on his face but his voice held concern as he brought his hand up to rest his palm against my cheek.

"What about you? Are you okay?"

I thought about his question and gave him an honest answer.

"Yes. I don't know what tonight meant and I am terrified of why some crazed man, well vampire given his powers has it out for me but I feel like everything will be okay. I don't have to lie to my best friend anymore and you have been great."

He smiled at me and nodded as he drew me into his chest for a hug. I breathed in the clean scent of him and wrapped my arms around him to hug him back. In that moment, I felt safe. Earlier that night I had been terrified but standing there with Lucas, it didn't matter. When he pulled away I looked up at him and was getting ready to say goodbye when spoke.

"Sophie, I wanted to ask you something."

"Okay. Shoot."

"Prom is coming up and I know it's a big deal for people these days. I have never been to one but I understand the concept and I think I would very much like to go with you. Would you accompany me?"

My smile was so big, my cheeks hurt. I hadn't given much thought to prom but now that he had asked, there was nothing I wanted to do more.

"Absolutely!"

He smiled and leaned down to kiss me on the forehead and when he pulled back he was wearing a happy expression.

"Okay. Go home now and get some rest. Just remember to be careful. I still don't know what's going on but we'll find out."

I nodded and headed to my car, happy.

CHAPTER 9

Prom night I stood in my room watching out the
window. It had been a few weeks since Lucas had
asked me to be his date but my excitement hadn't
worn off. To my dismay he still hadn't declared his
feelings for me but we spent almost every day
together and he was as attentive as any boyfriend,
so I let it be. Nora knew the truth about me and I
hadn't seen Daire since his run in with Lucas at the
coffee shop. Although we hadn't found any answers
to the past events, nothing strange or life
threatening had happened either and I had been
practicing my powers every chance I got. I seemed
to be building stamina because I could do more
magic without getting as tired. I had even learned to
levitate people when Nora had volunteered as a
test subject. The terrifying vampire with cold black
eyes still popped into my mind sometimes but it
was hard to worry when everything else in my life
seemed to be headed down the right track. I walked
over to my mirror to check myself out. I had no
shame in admitting that I was beautiful. My dress
was red satin with a halter top. It flowed over my
body hugging my curves. The back dipped to the
small of my back and the rounded neck in front was
accented with rhinestones. It fell almost to the floor,
letting my strappy, silver heels peek out. My nails
were done with French tips and a trip to the salon
earlier that day had resulted in my hair being piled
on my head in a curly mass with a few tendrils

escaping. Hearing a car I rushed to the window and saw that Lucas had arrived. I made my way down the stairs and as I stepped onto the porch he was coming up the steps. He paused at seeing me and I did a small twirl.

"What do you think?"

"You're beautiful, as always."

His voice was honest and he had an appreciative sparkle in his eyes. He was wearing a black suit with a red vest and tie. His wavy brown hair had been styled to perfection.

"You're not so bad yourself, very dashing. Are you up for pictures before we leave? My mom will never let me get out of here without them. Not to mention, she is dying to meet you."

"I'd be happy to."

I breathed out in relief. My mom had been pestering me to meet Lucas since I admitted that I was spending time with him. He walked up to meet and crooked his elbow in my direction. I slid my arm through his and we turned to head inside when I thought of something.

"Ummm.....will you show up in the pictures?"

It felt like a silly question but I had never asked him about it before. He let out a chuckle.

"Yes, that's just another myth."

With that, we headed inside to meet my mom. I found her and Bailey in the living room watching cartoons. Seeing me in the doorway with Lucas, she jumped up from the couch, grabbing her camera from the cushion beside her. Bailey was too engrossed in cartoons to really notice as my mom headed toward us.

"Aww...Honey! You look beautiful!"

She had helped me pick out the dress and had seen my hair but wanting her to be surprised, I had shooed her out of my room before I had done my make-up and put the dress on.

"Thanks mom." I motioned toward Lucas as I continued. "This is Lucas."

She looked over to him and her smile didn't diminish. She even had the audacity to wink at me. I let out a giggle as she held out her hand to Lucas. They shook hands quickly as she addressed him.

"It's nice to finally meet you! Sophie has been keeping you from me like a secret. I don't want you guys to be late, so I won't grill you tonight but I expect you two to behave and you have to come back soon so I can learn more about the boy who has been taking up all my daughter's free time!"

I looked over at Lucas to see his reaction. He smiled warmly at her and was nodding when he answered.

"Yes ma'am. We won't get into any trouble and I'll have her back at a decent time. Don't worry."

The smile that was plastered to my face grew even wider and my mom started ushering us around for pictures and Bailey even managed to ignore cartoons long enough to come take a few with us. After a few more compliments from my mom and even a few from Bailey, we made it out the door.

As we walked arm and arm into the gym of the school, I was surprised. It had been transformed. Where before it was a typical high school gym, now the ceiling looked like a starry sky and the walls were covered with white hangings. A dance floor had been created in the center and was edged by tables that were covered in blue cloths and surrounded by matching covered chairs. Some people were dancing and other's lounged at covered tables or milled around the food tables that had been set up on one side. There was also an ice sculpture of the school logo and a DJ station with music blaring from it. Taking in the scene, I remembered that theme was a masquerade ball. I brought the mask I was clutching up and put it on. I had searched all over Splendor for the perfect mask but not finding one I had resorted to internet shopping. I was happy with the results. It was a silver mask that curved over my face from the tip of my nose to halfway up my forehead. The edges were done in red edging and the bulk of it was decorated in swirling red and white lines. My favorite part was the red flower that sat on the edge of one side. It was what had set it apart from all the others I had looked at. Looking to my left at Lucas I saw that he had put his on as well. He had chosen a white mask that had gold trim around the edges and was covered in decorative, red, curving lines. Somehow, he pulled the look off. Looking at the other students, some of them looked a bit silly, but Lucas wore his with a confidence that made it seemed like he was made to wear it. I heard a familiar laugh and when I turned toward my arms were immediately filled with Nora.

"SOPHIE! You look amazing! I can't believe we made it to senior prom! This is going to be a blast!"

Before I could answer she had hold of my hand dragging me toward the dance floor with Lucas gliding behind us.

It seemed like a million songs later when we took a refreshment break. Lucas was an excellent dancer. He had surprised me when he joined us on the floor for a rap song. Who knew 100 year old

105

vampires could hip hop dance? We were headed for the punch bowl when "I'll be" by Edwin McCain flooded through the speakers. It was one of my all-time favorites and I gave Lucas a questioning look. He turned to me and bowed a little, extending his hand. When I placed my palm in his he gave the back of my hand a peck and led me to toward the dance floor. We had almost made it to the edge of the other dancers when I heard his phone ring. I looked at him questioningly. I had never heard or seen him get a phone call, so it was strange. He answered it with a quick hello and then covered the mouth piece to speak to me.

"I'm sorry; can you excuse me for a minute?"

I nodded and he made his way to the door leading outside. After he disappeared, I turned back to the dance floor. I saw Nora dancing with her date. She had her head on his shoulder and was obviously happy. I couldn't help but smile at her happiness. I heard a voice from behind me.

"May I have this dance?"

When I turned toward the voice, I saw a man dressed in a black suit. Even the tie and shirt were black. His mask was black too, with a twirled texture. His black hair was wavy and a few locks fell over his forehead. I recognized the voice and the man. No one else I knew carried themselves with such assurance, it was Daire. I looked around for Lucas but not seeing him, I decided to accept. When I nodded, he took my hand and led me to the dance floor. He pulled me close and wrapped one arm around my waist and held my hand out with his other. We started to sway to the music and I looked up to his face. I could see his blue eyes shining from behind the mask. What was he doing here? I wanted to know but I couldn't bring myself to break the moment and ask him. I was comfortable in his arms. I gave up wondering and rested my head on his shoulder, closing my eyes and breathing him in. When the last verses on the song began, I looked up at him again and was startled. His eyes were intense and determined as he leaned down toward me and released my hand to bring both of his hands to the sides of my face and hold it gently. I knew what was coming and I had no urge to fight it. I wanted it to happen; I didn't give a single thought to where we were or who might be watching. I felt his cool lips press to mine and heat rushed through me. Everything, even the music, faded away and the only thing I was aware of was his lips on mine. It was the kind of kiss you dream about and then abruptly, it was over. He pulled away from me and his hands left my face. I stood dazed for a second and realized that he had faded away into the crowd. Coming back to myself, I remembered Lucas. I looked around for him, desperately hoping he hadn't seen. Not seeing him anywhere, I made my way to a nearby chair and sat down. Was I out of my mind? Why did I kiss Daire? I liked Lucas and he made me happy; how could I do that to him? Should I tell Lucas? That answer was easy; definitely not. Maybe I would tell him later but I knew when I did he would react badly and I didn't want the night ruined. I was still mentally scalding myself when Lucas walked up. He was smiling when he arrived in front of me and I took that to mean he hadn't seen me with Daire and said silent thanks. I plastered a smile on my face and pushed Daire to the back of my mind as I placed my hand in Lucas's, determined to enjoy the rest of the night.

It was after midnight when we pulled into my driveway. I had successfully managed to make it through senior prom. I had enjoyed the dancing and had a great time but my dance and kiss with Daire was weighing on my mind. The rest of the night had went off without a hitch and I seemed to be the only one who knew what had transpired but it had me questioning my feelings. Part of me felt guilty for letting it happen and then not telling Lucas about it but a small slightly petty part of me thought it didn't matter. Lucas and I had never claimed each other as more than friends; did that mean I was allowed to kiss whoever I wanted? After thinking on it all night, I knew I had to say something. It didn't matter if we were a couple or not I felt wrong for not telling him and I knew I would feel that way until I came clean. I still wasn't sure why I had let Daire kiss me in the first place. All I knew was that I had wanted him to and not once did I stop to think of what a bad idea it was. It scared me to think that my feelings for Daire would be strong enough to completely override what I felt for Lucas. I knew what I needed to do to settle my mind and I wasn't looking forward to it. When Lucas killed the engine of the car I turned in my seat to face him and took a shaky breath before I spoke.

"Lucas, I want to ask you something."

He looked a little surprised but responded with a smile.

"Sure...anything."

"Well.....we have been hanging out a lot and I really like you. You're sweet and caring and I am glad that I have you in my life but....I guess...I was just wondering what this is between us. I didn't want to push our relationship but it's been over a month and I can't really get a handle on things."

I sat chewing my lip and waiting for his response. His face was pointed toward his lap when he answered in a resigned tone.

"I should have brought this up before now but I was enjoying spending time with you so much that I kept putting it off. Sophie, you're amazing and having you in my life is the best thing that has happened to me in a very long time. You look at me and see a person with feelings instead of a monster; you accepted me. For that, I'll be forever grateful and I value the friendship we have more than anything but it's impossible for it to be more. I shouldn't have kissed you, I know that. You are just so beautiful and I have feelings for you that I didn't even experience as a human, much less a vampire. I was wrong to kiss you and to keep kissing you. I wish it were different but it's not. In a few years, I'll have to leave here. People will start to notice that I'm not aging and it will be time for me to go. You deserve so much more than that; more than me. I love you Sophie and that's why we can't ever be anything more than friends."

My heart plummeted. I had thought about him leaving a handful of times but I always managed to push it away and concentrate on the present. He loved me? I didn't think I had ever been in love and wasn't even sure I would know if I was. Did I love him back? I had no idea. Did it matter? No, I would never have a real relationship with him, no matter how much I wanted it. For the first time in my life I had my heart broken.

I could feel the tears welling in my eyes and my throat started to close and I knew I was going to cry. Not wanting him to see me cry and not having anything to say to him, I flung open the car door and ran into my house. I was relieved that he didn't follow me as hot tears ran down my cheeks. I was glad to notice that my mom was already in bed and I wouldn't have to face her. I made my way to my room and crawled onto my bed, still wearing my dress and shoes. I stopped fighting the tears and cried until I drifted into sleep

CHAPTER 10

The next morning, I woke slowly. Usually, I was a morning person but after my crying jag the night before, I was anything but cheerful. I sat up and rubbed the sleep from eyes and I realized that I was still wearing my prom dress. So much for a great senior prom! I crawled out of bed and headed for the shower needing it to wake up and anxious to get out the dress.

After my shower, I threw on a pair of distressed blue jean shorts and a baby blue tee with matching flip flops and headed out the door. I didn't want to be at home. Memories of the night before wouldn't leave me alone and I wanted a peaceful place to think. Lucas's warning not to go off alone ran through my head but I wasn't interested in doing anything he asked anymore. I hopped into my car and started driving without a destination in mind. My heart was hurting, my head was full and I needed to sort through it all. I was eighteen years old but this was the first time I had wanted a serious relationship with someone and it was the first time they had rejected me. Over the years I had watched teen drama on television and almost laughed, thinking it was exaggerated but experiencing heart break for myself I realized that it really was that bad. I was more upset than I had ever been with the exclusion of losing my father. Thinking of my father gave me a destination. I headed across town toward Lake Splendor. When I got there, I knew I had come to the right place. My dad had taken me fishing there every year from as long as I could remember until he died. It held a lot of memories for me and I felt close to him there. My dad had been the kind of man that I could talk to about anything and I knew he would never judge me. He would offer advice and tell me that I could handle anything. I got out of the car and crunched across the gravel lot until I had made my way down to the edge of the lake. My inner turmoil seemed to be seeping out of my skin making it hot to the touch and the breeze coming in from the lake felt wonderful. I stood on the bank with eyes closed and breathed deeply. Just being there I felt like a weight had lifted. I started to walk along the water's edge thinking it all over for what seemed like the thousandth time. He had told me that he loved me. When you love someone aren't you supposed to want to be with them no matter what the odds are? I finally resigned myself to getting over it. It would be hard but I would do it. Lucas was right. He would have to leave and I couldn't and wouldn't go with him. I could never leave my mom and Bailey like that. It still hurt to think that after everything Lucas had helped me through that he wouldn't be there. He had been a source of comfort throughout everything. He walked me through Vampires 101, had supported me when I learned I was a witch and reassured me when I was attacked. He had been everything I needed him to be. I felt almost selfish thinking about it. Was I hurt because I truly wanted him to be around or was I sad that he wouldn't be there every time I needed someone? Grudgingly I admitted that it was both. Looking around, I realized that I had walked almost a mile from my car. I spun around to head back and that is when I saw her. Standing on the sandy bank in front of me was a woman. She was old, I guessed her to be at least 60. She was wearing a simple white dress that was something straight out of the past. Her gray hair was wrapped up in a bun and her eyes were the exact same shade as my own. I noticed an ethereal glow coming off of her. Deep down inside me I knew inexplicably, that she wasn't human but I felt connected to her. She was standing still, smiling when I spoke.

"Who are you?"

When she answered, it was with a melodious yet slightly raspy voice.

"I'm your great grandmother."

I was stunned for a second but came around quickly. I didn't necessarily believe her but given everything I had recently learned, I knew anything was possible. The old woman didn't make me feel threatened at all; actually it was quite the opposite. I decided to hear her out.

"Great grandmother? How is that possible and what are you doing here?"

"I am your father's grandmother, although he never knew me. In life, I was what is considered to be a witch. The power you have was passed down from me."

In life? If she wasn't alive then what was she?

"Are you an angel?"

"That is not important. The rules prevent me from telling you about what is on the other side. I came here to help you but I only have so much time. Listen hard Sophie, I know you have questions but I will tell you everything you need to know. I will start at the beginning... Almost 100 years ago, I lived in Splendor. One day a very powerful vampire, Cassian and his lover came to the town. His lover was named Eydis and was an empath demon. Meaning, she fed on the energy of those around her, eventually killing them. When the townspeople started dying mysteriously, I performed spells to find out why. In doing so, I discovered the true nature of Cassian and Eydis, and I knew that they were responsible. Spying on them, I learned that Splendor is the location of a hidden portal. It's a portal to a hell dimension and Eydis wanted to open it. She wanted to release a demon army for her to command. She wanted power. They had been taking the lives of Splendor's townspeople to make themselves powerful enough to open the portal. I tried to alert the townspeople but no one believed me. Cassian and Eydis had made friends with the town leaders and I had no proof of my claims. The townspeople thought I had gone mad and they locked me up, afraid that I was possessed. The night Eydis planned to open the portal I escaped and went to the location of the portal on the edge of the lake. Hidden in the trees, I performed a spell. I wasn't strong enough to destroy Eydis but I managed to entomb her inside Splendor rock."

The old woman gestured to the far bank of the lake and my eyes followed. There, on the edge of the bank, was Splendor Rock. It was a massive boulder, the edge of it jutting out into the lake. The surface was deep gray and had been worn smooth after years of erosion. When my eyes came back to her, she continued her story.

"To break the spell, one would need my blood or the blood of my living descendant and they would have to wait no less than 100 years. When I cast the spell on Eydis, Cassian fled into the night, promising to return for her. This June 5th at 11:00pm, exactly a hundred years will have passed and the spell can be broken. If Eydis is released, she will take out her vengeance on the town. Many people will die, and even more after she opens the portal. Cassian cannot be allowed to release her. I have seen you struggling. You had no knowledge of your power because after entombing Eydis, I ran away from Splendor. If I stayed I would have eventually been executed for being possessed. I left my husband and daughter behind and not knowing about my power they couldn't pass the secret on. You are ill prepared but you are the only one who has the power to defeat Cassian. You have to master your power and your heart to succeed. The blood used to break the spell must be from my descendant but for it to work my descendant must be alive when the unbinding spell is cast. This will offer you some protection until then but have no doubt that Cassian will kill you at the first opportunity."

My mind was reeling. I could feel the truth in her words. I was expected to save people from a demon and prevent a hell army from coming to earth? I couldn't even manage to get a vampire to date me and now people's lives depended on me. No pressure, right? Her story did offer explanation for my being attacked. I grew even more depressed when I realized that Cassian already had my blood. He was the one I had met after my day of shopping with Nora. The old woman stood, watching me intently. My mind was buzzing and I couldn't find what I wanted to say. Finally, the words were there.

"How am I supposed to defeat him? I barely know how to use my powers and he already has my blood. The last time I met him, my power didn't even come close to his."

I was a little ashamed at the whininess in my voice. This woman had given up everything to save others and here I was feeling sorry for myself. I was preparing to apologize when she spoke.

"Sophie, you have yet to tap into your full power and there is much for you to learn. You have figured out how to use your will to make things happen but it is not enough. You have to embrace who you are. Your lack of acceptance keeps you from reaching your full potential. You have to want the magic and be confident in your abilities. Being strong earns you strong power, it isn't given. Don't overlook the power you have in other areas either. You're a good girl and others see the good in you. You should embrace the relationships you have and the strength and support others will give. You have powerful allies. Is there not a vampire in your life, who cares for you deeply? Who would give everything for you?"

I was confused. My first thought was of Lucas but remembering my dance with Daire, the night before, I was hesitant to say.

"Are you talking about Lucas?"

"Sophie, I cannot give you all the answers. You will find the answers that you need as long as you have the courage to follow your heart."

The light around her began to quiver and her face reflected alarm. She reached out and took my hand in hers as she continued.

"My time here is almost up. Your blood, when freely given, can share your power with another. You only have to want it. Choose wisely. Not everyone is who they seem and if you choose wrong you will lose everything."

As she said the last, the wavering light grew faint and then she was gone. The hand she had been holding dropped to my side at her sudden disappearance. I looked around me but there was nothing to show she had been there. The lake was quiet and calm and the ground where she had stood didn't reveal any sign of her. I trudged back to my car, the peace I had felt on arrival was broken and my mind was on overload. Not only was I expected to save lives with powers I wasn't quite sure how to use but then there was her cryptic remark about choosing. I got the point that I could share my magic with someone else if I willingly gave them my blood but who was I supposed to give it to. I eliminated everyone besides Lucas and Daire immediately, who else would drink my blood? How was I going to choose between them? I was leaning toward Lucas based on my feelings alone. Try as I might, I couldn't stop liking him just because he had told me we couldn't be together, especially since I saw some truth in his words. Grandmother had said someone wasn't who they seemed and I couldn't imagine Lucas lying to me. He had been honest with me about everything from the very beginning but thinking of the night before, the last thing I wanted to do was see Lucas. Of course, I couldn't ignore Daire either. His actions the night before had made certain of that. When I was in sight of my car, I sat down in a patch of grass at the edge of the water. What was I going to do? Everything had gone downhill in the blink of an eye and there was so much depending on my actions. I lay back in the grass and closed my eyes, feeling the sunshine on my face. Without warning, tears sprung from my eyes and soon I was lying in the grass bawling. It was all too over whelming. I didn't want to be responsible for other people. I couldn't handle it if I failed. With no one around to see, I let the tears come. When I was all cried out, I lay there emotionally exhausted and sunk into sleep.

When I woke there was a chill in the air. Groggily, I sat up. I looked around and seeing the sun was low in the sky realized I had slept for a while. I started to rise and noticed my favorite hoodie was draped over me. How did it get there? I hadn't worn it in weeks and the last I had seen, it was in the back of my car. I definitely hadn't been wearing it earlier. Beside me, I saw the rose. It was long stemmed with deep pink petals. Daire. It unnerved me to realize that he had been around while I was sleeping and totally vulnerable. Not willing to face any more feelings that day, I scooped up the rose and headed home, trying to forget.

CHAPTER 11

I was sitting on my bed trying to concentrate on my homework and it wasn't working. I sighed in frustration and tossed the pen and notepad down beside me. Nora looked up from the book she was reading at my desk with a quizzical expression.

"Having trouble?"

"Yea, I've been in the twilight zone all day. I can't focus on anything."

Nora's face was sympathetic. I had told her about my experience at the lake yesterday as well as after prom. However, I was still keeping my kiss with Daire a secret. She had offered to come over after school and I had readily accepted, grateful for the distraction.

"Sorry, Soph. I wish I could say that I can relate but I'd be lying. I don't really know what to tell you."

"How about 'you're not crazy'."

She laughed even though it was a poor attempt at humor.

"You're not crazy! I know it all sucks but there must be a silver lining somewhere. You just have to find it."

For the first time, her optimism didn't make me feel better.

"I don't see how this could possibly have an upside. Let's see, my dead great-grandmother appeared and informed me that I am now responsible for the lives of a lot of people against a super powerful vampire who is hell bent on releasing a power hungry psychotic demon. To top it off, Lucas simultaneously confessed his love and rejected me right after I kissed Daire, the vampire who tried to kill me."

Nora's mouth was hanging open. Oops! I hadn't meant to let that last bit slip. I cringed, knowing that there was no way she was going to let it go.

"WHAT?! You kissed Daire?"

Her face showed that she was hurt and I realized it was confession time.

"Umm...yea. Sorry! With everything else that's going on, I wasn't ready to deal with that yet so I didn't mention it."

"Well, you've let it slip now. You might as well go ahead and spill it all."

Nora's expression was still slightly wounded but I knew she understood why I hadn't told her. I gave her a complete rundown of my dance and subsequent kiss with Daire. By the end, any annoyance she had felt was gone and replaced with a dreamy look in her eyes.

"Wow that is romantic."

"Romantic? He tried to kill me and now I am kissing him! It seems more like a case of dementia."

"Did you enjoy kissing him?"

"Definitely."

I had answered without hesitation but when I saw the wicked gleam in her eye, I wished I could take it back.

"Interesting. Is he hot?"

I half snorted and half laughed. I should have anticipated that response.

"Do I have to be honest?"

She lowered her brows and gave me a stern look.

"Okay. Okay. Yes. He is gorgeous."

She leaned forward wearing an eager expression.

"Do tell."

I should have known she'd get around to asking eventually. Actually, I was surprised it had taken her that long. With Nora it was usually one of the first questions when a guy was mentioned.

"Well, he is tall with dark hair and he has blue eyes that seem to go on for miles."

"Oooh! So what are you going to do about it?"

"About what?"

"Daire. I mean I agree that it's was a little wrong to kiss him but I'm not here to judge and after the Lucas love confession and rejection fiasco, it doesn't really matter. So are you going to try to snag him or not? I'm voting for snagging, he sounds like a dream."

"A dream? Did you miss the part where he attacked me and sucked out all my blood?"

"Nope but apparently you guys are over that stage in your friendship. Plus, it must not matter to you all that much if you are sucking face with him."

What?! That was crazy. Actually, it wasn't. As usual, Nora had managed to take a complicated thing and lay out the facts that lay at the heart of the situation. She looked smug as she watched me figure it out.

"Okay, you've got me there. That still doesn't mean I want to 'snag' him, far from it. He feeds on people! I feel a little disgusted with myself when I remember I kissed a killer and enjoyed it."

"Okay but you were all for Lucas and he admitted that he has killed people."

"I know but I guess....I just think about it differently because he changed. He wants to be a good person. It's hard for me to judge someone on their past when they are trying so hard to make it right."

"If you say so. You do realize that eventually you're going to have to choose one of them, right?" She gave me a blatant stare. One more thing I could rely on Nora for was making me face my problems...even when I didn't want to.

I hesitated but knowing Nora wasn't going to give it a rest, I answered.

"I don't know. I could just forget them both and handle this myself."

Nora's face showed shock that quickly turned to disapproval.

"Okay, Sophie. Now you're crazy!"

"Why?"

"You can't face that Cassian guy alone! He was wicked scary and your grandma made it pretty clear that if this goes badly, you can die! I wish you didn't have to do this at all but since you do, you better use all the help you can get! I would never forgive you if you got yourself killed!"

"I guess....." My voice trailed off. I knew this wasn't an argument I could win.

"I'm serious Sophie! If you don't get around to asking at least one of them for help, I'll ask them myself!"

Her face was deadly serious and I knew she meant every word.

"How do I choose? They could die for helping me! Not to mention, the cryptic remarks my grandma made about people not being who they seem. How am I supposed to know who to trust?"

She started grinning again as she replied.

"Your grandma also said to follow your heart, Soph. It's simple. Pick the one you love."

"I don't think I'm in love with either of them! I've never even been in love, how am I supposed to know?" I ran my fingers up through my hair in frustration. I had been having this same conversation in my head all day and I still didn't have any answers.

"I don't know but you've got a little over a month to figure it out."

"Gee thanks. No pressure, right?"

"Sorry, just being honest. It's one of my many services." Nora said as she gave me a wink.

In spite of myself, I smiled as she continued.

"So what are you going to do about the Lucas situation in the meantime? I mean, it's not like you can ignore him forever. Plus, you should probably talk to him since you might be asking for his help later."

"I don't know. I don't know anything and I'm not really ignoring him. It's not my fault he didn't come to school."

I dropped my head into my hands, sighing.

Nora's smile fell and she leaned forward in her chair to give me a reassuring pat on the back. "Don't worry, Soph. We'll figure it out."

I lifted my head and smiled at her. I knew I could trust her, always. We had a friendship that only comes around once in a lifetime. She knew me better than anyone and if anyone could help me sort this mess out, it was her.

"Thanks."

"I think you should start by talking to Lucas. You can't expect to make a good decision if you guys are on the outs."

I sighed again. "You're right."

She gave me a wicked grin.

"Of course, I am."

In spite of myself, I was smiling as I picked up the phone to call Lucas.

CHAPTER 12

I paced the parking lot of the reserve anxiously. I had spoken to Lucas for only a minute the day before when I called and asked him to meet me. He had been absent from school again and I was nervous. What should I say to him? Before I could finish working it out, I saw his mustang pull into the lot. I took a few deep breaths to calm myself and casually crossed my arms, not wanting him to know how unsure I was feeling. I watched him park and head my way as he exited his car. My heart clenched in my chest. He was so handsome and everything I could want in a boyfriend but I knew I could never have him. In the openness of the parking lot I felt exposed; I headed for the woods, hoping I would feel more guarded. Inside the tree line, I stopped and waited for him to catch up. When he had come to stand beside me I continued walking the dirt path and awkwardly started to speak.

"Look, I understand that we can't be together. Your reasoning makes sense. Can we be friends?"

I was making an effort to be blunt and to the point. I didn't think beating around the bush would help our situation or my emotional state.
He looked taken aback. Obviously, he wasn't expecting that. His answer was hesitant.

128

"Yea……..of course."

There was an awkward pause and I made no effort to fill the silence, so he continued.

"I'm sorry for what I did. It wasn't my intention to hurt you. I didn't mean to fall in lov……"

"DON'T SAY IT!"

I cut him off. I knew where his words were going and I had no interest in visiting that particular subject. Regardless of our feelings, we couldn't be together and there wasn't any point in exploring something I could never have. His face looked hurt and I had an almost uncontrollable urge to kiss him. Instead, I continued more calmly.

"I'm sorry….I just don't want to talk about that. I don't need to know all that to be friends. I accept your apology and that's enough."

He gave a reluctant nod. I wondered if I should fill him in on everything that I had learned since prom. I looked at his face and I didn't see anything but sincerity and everything was on the tip of my tongue ready to spill out when I caught myself. I wouldn't tell him. I just didn't want to. Maybe, I was just being petty because I was upset but it wasn't going to change my mind. Noticing, that I was studying him, he gave a puzzled expression that

129

quickly turned to hopefulness. I gave a weak smile and turned to him, sticking my hand out.

"Friends?"

He smiled back and took my hand in his. He shook briefly and let it drop, turning to walk back toward our cars. It was almost symbolic.

His voice was steady when he said "Friends."

I thought I would feel better after making things right with him but I didn't. I had considered just cutting him out of my life completely but I knew that I might need him. It sounded awful even to me. I knew I was using him in a sense but it was what I had to do until I figured out how to handle Cassian. I knew being friends with him was going to be hard, considering my feelings but if it helped me figure out the mess I was in, I was willing to do it. Having settled our issue, I moved toward an easier conversation.

"So……Why weren't you at school?"

He looked at his feet as he walked.

"I figured you might not want to see me."

He was right. I hadn't wanted to see him but I shook my head.

"I'll admit, I was a little upset but I really do want to be friends."

And I did. I just wanted the friendship we had before and I knew it was gone. Reaching the parking lot, he gave me a rueful glance.

"I'm glad. I hate to run but I have an errand to do. See you tomorrow at school?"

"Yea, for sure." The cheerfulness in my tone was hollow.
There was a pause as we stood there, not knowing what to do. Then he gave me a wink and walked away. I was still standing in place when his car left the parking lot. I let out a deep breath. Things may have been settled with Lucas but I definitely didn't feel any relief. Friends or not, I knew that things weren't going to get any easier for me. I still had decisions to make and I had no idea where to begin. When I turned to get into my car, I caught myself standing face to face with Daire. Obviously, my day was only going to get more difficult! A smile played across his lips and I felt my head spin at the sight of him. No matter how many times I had seen him before, I was still somewhat stunned by his beauty.

"Hello Blondie."

"Hi Daire."

I wasn't sure what to say to him. The last time I had seen him, we had kissed so I was feeling awkward and with all the emotions I had running through me over Lucas, I just wasn't feeling up our usual banter. Daire was ,as usual, relaxed and casual.

"Another date with the Golden boy?"

"No. It wasn't a date."

He looked briefly puzzled and then his normal cocky grin was back in place.

"Trouble in paradise?"

I was irritated that he would ask and the scowl on my face showed it. He put both of his hands up as if in surrender and I realized that I might as well tell him. How much worse could it make things?

"Yea...you could say that. I was pretty naive to think we could make it work wasn't I?"

I felt awkward asking him relationship questions but I knew that he wouldn't sugar coat the answer.

"Blondie, I'm not really sure what happened but I wouldn't call you naïve. I'd call it hopeful and there is nothing wrong with having hope."

It was the nicest thing he had ever said to me. He usually played the part of dark and mysterious perfectly but today there was openness in his face that I hadn't seen before.

"Uh....Thanks."

He put his hands in the pocket of his jeans and casually reclined against my Explorer. His face was unreadable as I got caught up in looking at him. His navy button up showed off the muscles in his throat and it's rolled sleeves highlighted his sculpted for arms. As usual, he looked like he stepped off the cover of GQ. I was upset but how could I help but appreciate the view?

"So, what are you going to do about your date with Cassian?"

As his words sank in, I shook my head. All I could think was 'huh?' Instead of revealing my shock I calmly said "How do you know about that?".

"I was at the lake."

He answered simply, as if it should have been obvious. I felt anger flush through me and my voice came out much louder than I intended.

"YOU WERE SPYING ON ME?"

Unfazed by the fury in my tone, He shrugged as he answered.

"If that's how you want to see it."

"You have no right!"

"Be that as it may....you still haven't answered my question."

I closed my eyes and took a few deep breaths. I was supremely pissed that he invaded my privacy. He was basically stalking me and I felt violated. I heard nothing out of him as I struggled for composure. As mad as I was, it did solve the issue of whether I should tell him or not. I was already feeling bad for leaving Lucas out of the loop. I swallowed my anger and answered but I could hear the annoyance in my voice.

"I don't know."

"That's not good, Blondie. You need to figure it out. Cassian is ruthless and Eydis isn't any better."
"Thanks but I had a pretty good idea of that already. How do you know about him?"

His ever present grin didn't falter as he answered. "I know a lot of things Blondie but that doesn't mean I am going to tell you."

I felt stupid for asking. I should have known he wouldn't tell me. My annoyance with him flared. "Why does all this matter to you anyways?"

His blue eyes bored into mine as he spoke.
"That's my own business."

Okay, fine. I stood, silently. Two could play his game.

"What about your blood?"

I sighed loudly. I should have known he would ask the question I least wanted to answer.

"I don't know."

"You say that a lot. Your choices are simple. There is only Lucas and I to choose from." It did sound simple but if I chose wrong, people would die, myself included.

"Yea, I got that. I guess you're forgetting that one of you isn't who they seem but I have no way of telling which one."

His face turned serious as he straightened and stepped forward, looking down into my face.

"You were told to follow your heart. What is it saying?"

It wasn't saying anything. It was thumping wildly in my chest. He was so close that if he had been human I would have felt the heat coming off of his skin and I could smell that wonderful scent that only belonged to him.

"It isn't saying anything." I sounded a little breathless but was relieved that my voice hadn't wavered. My adrenaline was flowing and I felt like I was on a runaway train. Him being so close affected me much more than I wanted it to.

He brushed a finger over my hair as he spoke. "Blondie you shouldn't lie, it doesn't become you."

Not having an answer for that and my heart still trying to beat out of my chest, I stood stock still, waiting.

"Do you believe I would lie to you?"

I answered honestly. He already knew so much that there was no point in lying or trying to evade.

"No but I don't think Lucas would lie to me either."

He looked irritated by my response but when he stepped back I felt relief. My heart slowed marginally. He scratched his chin, obviously thinking.

"You truly believe that Lucas wouldn't lie to you?" His response sounded more like an insult than a question but I answered anyways.

"Yes, that's what I just said."

"Get in the car."

"What?"

"Get in the car.
His tone wasn't angry or forceful. It was efficient and left no room for argument so I obeyed. When he climbed into the passenger side, I was slightly alarmed and a whole lot curious.

"Where are we going?"

"To fix a problem. Don't look so afraid.."

I wasn't afraid but not wanting to tell him that, I buckled up and started the car.

CHAPTER 13

"Pull off and park."

As I pulled off the side of the road, I realized that the short ride Daire and I had taken from the reserve had led us only yards from Lucas's driveway. I shut the car off and turned toward Daire.

"What are we doing here?"

"Stop asking questions and get out."

I huffed but did as he asked. My curiosity had been building since we left the reserve, making me ignore his rudeness. He had been silent during the ride other than to give directions and all my attempts at finding out our destination had been ignored. It was getting dark and there was a chill in the air even though it was already late April. My feet crunched across the ground as I walked to catch up with Daire, who was already headed to the driveway.

"Are we going to Lucas's? Why didn't we just drive up?"

He shot me an exasperated look.

"We didn't come for a social visit. Be quiet. Do you think Lucas would react well to my being here?"

That shut me up. I had a feeling that I really didn't want to know what we were up to but I was already neck deep into it. We walked the long driveway in silence. He had made a good point when he said Lucas wouldn't like him being there and I wasn't feeling up to seeing an argument. I had never gotten any information on why they had so much animosity toward one another and I hadn't pushed, a little afraid of what it might be. By the time we neared the end of the long driveway, it was full dark and my stomach was jumping but it was too late to turn back. I spotted Lucas's house with light coming through the windows to illuminate the darkness. I turned to Daire, ready to speak but he put a finger to his lips and kept walking. His pace slowed and his steps made not a single sound. I tried to mimic his movements but failed miserably. I could still hear my every footstep crunch. He shook his head and turned toward me, before I knew it he had scooped me up in his arms. He shot me a stern look and it silenced any protest I might have made. I was acutely aware of him as we walked. His all too familiar scent wrapped around me and I couldn't stop myself from breathing it in. It was a unique scent and it suited him perfectly, musky and dark. My heart started hammering in my chest as it did every time he got close to me. I hoped he wouldn't hear it but I knew it was wishful thinking.

Lucas had told me that vampires had amazing hearing and I couldn't imagine the sound of blood pumping would miss one's notice. I was caught up in trying to discreetly study the graceful curve of his throat when he stopped. He gently placed me on my feet and I realized that I was sad that he had let me go. I noticed that we were right outside of Lucas's living room window. With both of us slightly crouched, I gave Daire a panicked look. I knew we shouldn't be there. We were going to spy on him and it was wrong. Hadn't I just been upset with Daire for the same thing? Not to mention, if Lucas caught us our fragile friendship would probably be over. Daire rolled his eyes and put a finger over his lips. He definitely wasn't going anywhere. I briefly debated heading back to car but I wasn't keen on the idea of walking back through the dark alone and without Daire carrying me I was terrified that Lucas would hear me and I'd get caught anyways. I was stuck spying on him. Great. I decided to turn around and not participate but Daire grabbed me and pulled me up beside him. With just our eyes above the sill, I could see Lucas's living room through a gap in the curtains. Not seeing Lucas, I shot Daire an annoyed look. I wasn't sure what the point of all this was but I knew that I didn't want to stare at an empty room all night. His only reaction was to tip his head toward the window. I turned to stare in again. I would give it five more minutes for Daire to prove his point but after that I was leaving, with or without him. I stared into the window for a few minutes still seeing nothing but the empty room. I was wondering if five minutes had passed when Lucas walked in. He was smiling and he wasn't alone. Trailing behind him was a beautiful woman. She had flowing dark hair and large doe eyes. I wasn't close enough to see their color but I knew it was probably as marvelous as the rest of her. She had a wide mouth that was curved into an open mouthed smile as her voluptuous frame shook with laughter. I couldn't take my eyes off of them. Lucas had never mentioned having friends other than me. Quite the opposite, He had told me that he valued my friendship so much because it was the only one he had. I knew it was petty but I had enjoyed it. I jumped as Daire placed his hand on my back. I shot him a glance and he looked apologetic, something I hadn't believed was possible. I turned my attention back to the scene playing out in the living room. Lucas and the mystery woman had made it to the sofa and were sitting hip to hip. He had his arm around her shoulders and was running a finger down her cheek. I couldn't believe what I was seeing. He had rejected me because a relationship was impossible but it seemed that rule only applied to me. Maybe she was a vampire. I would still be upset but that would explain a little of it. I looked over at Daire and found his gaze on me, instead of the scene through the window. I held a hand in front of my mouth and made fangs with question in my eyes. Catching my question, he gave a small shake of his head. My heart sank. I pushed the hurt away, determined to keep watching. Maybe there was something else to

141

explain all this. It was never good to jump to conclusions. I watched as Lucas leaned forward to whisper in the woman's ear and then brush his lips over her cheek. Her eyes were closed and she wore a blissful expression. He trailed kisses over her face and down to her throat. Then, I saw his fangs. Before I could call out, I felt Daire's hand clamp down over my mouth and I watched as Lucas buried his fangs in the woman's neck. He began sucking at the wound he had made and blood trailed from his mouth, running down his chin and the woman's neck until it seeped into their shirt collars. The woman had her eyes open with a faraway look in them, apparently unaware of anything going on around her. She sat motionless, like stone. I felt the water start to well in my eyes and I squeezed them tightly shut. My whole opinion of Lucas had crumbled in a matter of seconds. Daire's hand was still clamped over my mouth and I pulled at it. Hesitantly, he dropped his hand. I turned and strode away into the dark, not caring if Lucas caught me spying on him. I had made it across the yard and to the driveway when I felt Daire walking beside me. I didn't acknowledge him. I continued walking, my purposeful footsteps resounding in the night. After a completely silent walk, we were back at my car. Wordlessly, we got in and I headed back into town. Finally, Daire spoke.

"I'm sorry but you had to know."

I was angry and incredulous. He was sorry? I didn't believe it.

"YOU'RE SORRY? YOU MADE ME WATCH THAT AND ALL YOU CAN SAY IS YOU'RE SORRY? WHY DID YOU GO THROUGH ALL THE TROUBLE? WHY NOT JUST TELL ME INSTEAD OF MAKING ME SEE IT?"

I hadn't meant to yell and I knew I was taking out my upset and frustration over Lucas on Daire but I didn't care. He had taken me there with the sole purpose of showing me that Lucas had lied to me. I would never get that image out of my head and I had Daire to thank for it. I had expected him to take my outburst as he did everything else, with cool indifference and I was surprised when his voice came out low and sounding wounded.

"Would you have believed me if I had told you?"

"Ye....."

My voice trailed off. He was right. I never would have believed it if I hadn't seen it.

"No."

He nodded, acknowledging my answer.

"Now what do you plan to do about Cassian?"
I hadn't even begun to think about what the night meant for me in regards to Cassian and I wasn't about to work through it with Daire.

"I don't know and I don't want to talk about it."

"Your choice is obvious."

"Huh?" It wasn't a very dignified response but it was all I had.

"Obviously, Lucas has been lying which leaves you stuck with me."

"That's what this was about?! You ruined my entire outlook on Lucas all so I would choose you?"

"In a way, yes."

"I wish I could say that I can't believe it but unfortunately I can."

I knew my voice had a vicious tone but I didn't care. I had had enough. I looked over at him.

"Why?"

"Blondie, it's obvious you're attracted to me. You were always going to choose me. I just helped you make the decision faster."

I was speechless. I had never heard a more arrogant statement. I could admit that I was attracted to him but I definitely hadn't chosen him and I still might not. I gathered my wits and alternated between glaring at him and concentrating on the road.

"You're wrong."

A smug smile slid across his face.

"About which part? You being attracted to me or you choosing me?

I wanted to deny it all but I knew it would be childish.

"About choosing you. My being attracted to you is irrelevant."

He raised an eyebrow and the air around him practically hummed with arrogance. Something inside me snapped. I was tired of playing this game with him and I was beyond tired of having my life turned upside down. I didn't know what I was going to do but I knew that someone else wasn't going to make the decision for me. I slammed on the brakes and swerved to the shoulder of the road. I could hear rocks flying out from under the tires and pinging off my SUV. When we had stopped completely, I turned toward him, my face furious.

"Get out!"

His smile slipped for a second but was quickly back in place. I didn't know if he would obey me or not and I was afraid I would have to use my powers to get him out of the car but silently, he opened the door and stepped into the night. He turned and gave me a wink. Infuriated, I gunned the engine and my car sped forward. He stepped back as I did and the open door slammed shut from the momentum. I didn't bother looking back. I managed to get home and make it upstairs to my room before I started crying.

I sat at the lunch table, slouched in my seat. I was staring at my plate of untouched food listening to Nora ramble on about her morning classes. No matter how hard I tried, I just couldn't bring myself to be interested. I was feeling sorry for myself and I knew it but even Nora hadn't been able to cheer me up after the weekend's events. I was pissed at Daire for setting me up and I was hurt by Lucas's lies but mostly I was just depressed that I wasn't any closer to finding an answer on how to deal with Cassian. I had thought about finding him and dealing with him alone but deep down I knew I wasn't ready to face him. No matter how much I practiced with my powers it never seemed to be enough to compare with his and alone in my thoughts I could admit that I was deathly afraid of him. I didn't want to die. I was only eighteen. I was supposed to have an entire life ahead of me and knowing that it could be taken from me made me feel defeated already. I had filled Nora in on everything but she couldn't really offer help. For her it was simple....I should just choose someone and jump in head first. I knew that's how she would handle it but I just couldn't bring myself to see it that way. I cared about Lucas more than I had cared about any other guy whether he lied to me or not and my first instinct told me to choose him but Daire would always dance into my mind. He was cryptic and I didn't really know anything about him other than that he was a murderer and occasionally stalked me. Not exactly star qualities but something within me trusted him. Yet, at the same time, his behavior made me suspicious. He had gone to great lengths to make sure I chose him, but why? What did he have to gain from it? I couldn't imagine him helping people out of the goodness of his heart but looking at the Lucas side of things, he had lied to me once and as unimaginable as it might be he could lie to me again. It was maddening to think about it over and over again but what choice did I have? My life depended on my decision and I couldn't seem to concentrate on anything else. My mom had noticed that I had been distant as well as Nora and my teachers. This was ruining my life and I hadn't even made a choice. How much worse would it be when I had made one? I wanted to live and this wasn't living. It was wallowing. That was how I came to a decision. I may not have known who to choose for help but I knew that if I might die, I wanted to squeeze as much life as I could into whatever time I had left. Cassian wouldn't come for me until after he released Eydis and by then I would have either stopped him or I would be dead so there wasn't a threat there. I wasn't going to think about this anymore until after graduation. That gave me roughly a month to live my life and then I would reevaluate everything. I believed in fate and whatever was supposed to happen would happen. Until then, I was going to live. I looked up at Nora and smiled. This was going to be fun.

CHAPTER 14

I sat in a metal folding chair on the school's football
field with the sun shining down on me. It was the
end of May and graduation day. I had spent the last
month doing whatever I wanted. Nora and I had
spent a weekend at the lake, I had a spa day with
my mom, and I had even taken Bailey to the zoo. I
had spent time with everyone who meant the most
to me and I had fun doing it. They weren't life
altering activities like climbing Mount Everest but it
was what was important to me.

My only complaint was that it was coming to
an end and soon I would have to make the decision
I had put off. Thoughts of Lucas, Daire, and the
situation with Cassian had tried to creep into my
mind over the last month but I shoved them away
refusing to deal with it. I could admit that I did miss
Lucas and Daire. I had seen Lucas around school
but even though we were friendly toward each
other it wasn't the same as before and I could
never erase the image of him feeding on that
woman from my mind. I had never confronted him
about that and I didn't plan to. It was his right to tell
me and he chose not to. Since I only saw him at
school, I would plaster a smile on my face and Nora
would do most of the conversing for us. I had
explained my decision to leave it all alone for a
while and she had hesitantly agreed. I was thankful
I had her to run interference.

As for Daire, I hadn't seen him since the
night I kicked him out of my car. I was a little

worried that he had left and I wouldn't have him if I needed him but I reminded myself that whatever happened was meant to happen and if that meant he was supposed to leave then so be it. At least my decision would be made for me, no matter how unsure I was about it.

Realizing all the other people on my row were standing, I shook myself from my thoughts and stood with them. As I walked toward the stage, my heart started pounding. I was graduating, with honors. I heard Nora's name called and I looked at her, beaming as she crossed the stage to accept her diploma. My heart continued to pound as they called out more names. Finally, I heard my name and started my walk across the stage. I could hear my mom yelling from the crowd seated in the stadium. I accepted my diploma and walked back to my seat to wait for the ceremony to end. I knew my fun filled month was over and I was glad it was ending with a bang. I was proud of myself. This was by far my biggest accomplishment yet. I only hoped I would be as successful with Cassian.

After the ceremony was over, My mom and Bailey had met me on the field along with Nora and her parents. A lot of hugs were exchanged and eventually I made it to the parking lot to head home. When I reached my Explorer I climbed in, tossing my stuff into the back seat. As I turned the key I noticed the single fuchsia colored rose lying in the passenger seat. I lifted it to my nose and inhaled its scent. Regardless of what was coming, I was happy.

CHAPTER 15

A few days later Nora and I were sitting on my bed. Her family was getting ready to leave for vacation like they did every summer and as usual Nora was hanging out with me on her last night before leaving. Neither of us had brought up what we were both thinking about. I knew it needed to be said but Nora got to it before I did.

"So, have you decided what you're going to do?"

"No."

"Sophie! That's not good. I know you wanted a break from it an all but it's crunch time. The 5th is tomorrow! You need to choose."

I sighed…She wasn't telling me anything I didn't already know. I rose from my bed and got up to pace.

"Nora, I know to you this seems so simple. I should just choose the one I love but I don't know which one that is. I barely know Daire and I don't know if what I had with Lucas was love or not. What if I choose wrong?"
Pensively, Nora sat for a moment before she spoke.

"Sophie I know it's hard. What if it isn't who you love but who you could grow to love?"

"What? I guess it could be that but I still don't know who to choose! I have never been in love! How am I supposed to know if I could love one of them or not? For all I know I could love them both!" I drug my hands through my hair, still pacing. After a month, my decision wasn't any clearer and to be honest, I was tired of having this debate. I had been over it time and time again and I was terrified of choosing wrong.

Nora's voice was soft when she spoke "Maybe you love them both."

Plopping down on the bed next to her, I felt defeated. "Maybe I do but again it doesn't help me decide. I know it's not your fault Nora. I'm sorry I am so frustrated."

She smiled and took my hand. "Sophie we are best friends and that's only because god knew our mother's couldn't handle us as sisters. I know you are frustrated and I know this is hard but you have to make a decision. I have every faith that you'll make the right decision."

I smiled at her. She really was the best friend I would ever have.

"Thanks. I know I am and have been a pain over this whole thing and I am glad you love me enough to overlook it. Don't worry. I'll figure this out. Go on your trip and have a good time. I'll be here when you get back." My eyes started tearing up as I spoke. I couldn't believe that this might be the last time I ever saw her.

"Are you sure? I told you I would stay behind and help you. I feel wrong running off and leaving you to deal with this." Her eyes were starting to water too.

"No. I told you, go have fun. There isn't much you can do to help and if I am worried about you I'll be useless. I would feel so much better knowing you are safe. Worrying about my mom and Bailey is enough."

Tears were flowing down her face as she nodded. She flung her arms around me as she said "Sophie, I know you can do it. Promise me you'll be here when I get back!"

Returning her hug and crying, I breathed out a quiet "I promise."

Nora left shortly after that and my heart broke. I hadn't decided what to do and knowing I was on my own until I made a decision weighed on me. I paced around my room for a while and unable to come up with anything new I called Lucas. When he answered, His voice was hesitant "Sophie..."

I steeled my voice and prepared to ask what I wanted to know.

"Look, I know we haven't been close lately but I have something I need to ask you."
Hearing only silence on the other end, I continued.

"Do you care about me?"
His voice was honest and his answer was immediate.

"Sophie, I more than care about you, I love you. There is just so much more to this than how I feel."
I knew I was going to cry. Partly, because the call hadn't helped me make my decision and partly, for what I could have had with Lucas and knew I never would.

My voice broke as I spoke "Thanks for being honest. That was all I needed to ask." With that, I ended the call.

I was sitting on the edge of my bed turning the phone over and over in my hands when I heard him speak.

"Why so blue?"

I jolted and looked around frantically. Glancing at my window, I realized Daire was right outside, his handsome face looking straight at me. My window was on the second story and even though I knew some vampires could levitate, I had never seen it. I couldn't help myself from asking.

"How are you standing out there?"

His mouth curved into a familiar grin as he answered.

"Levitation. You should try it sometime."

His cockiness never failed to bring out my annoyance and that night was no exception.

"I tried. It didn't work."

I hadn't tried out my powers a lot over the last month. I wanted to forget them along with everything else, even if it was only temporary. The few times I had tried to levitate myself had been failures. Nothing had happened. Daire's voice was serious as he responded.

"You didn't want it bad enough."

Not wanting to fight with him, I bit back the smart response that came to mind and instead said "Did you come here just to insult me or did you have a purpose?"

He faked a hurt expression as he said "Blondie, you wound me. I can't stop by and have a chat with a friend?"

I choked a little. "Friend? Is that what I am? You'll have to forgive me for being a little out of the loop, the last time I checked friends didn't try to kill each other."

"You're still holding that against me?"

He almost sounded peeved about it but I just didn't care. I wasn't really in the mood to deal with him at all. I huffed.

"Give me one good reason, why I shouldn't."

I crossed my arms, waiting for his response. He looked thoughtful.

"Because I care about you."

My breath caught. That was one of the last things I had expected him to say. I wasn't sure how to respond. So instead, I walked to the window and put my hands out to him. His face was curious as he took my hands and I pulled him into my room. He floated in effortlessly. When he was standing, both feet on the floor, I put my hands one each side of his face, stood on my tip toes and pulled his lips to mine. He stayed still as if he was in shock for a second and then his hands tangled in my hair and I felt his cool lips respond to mine. He tasted exotic and I felt a rush of heat course through me. It felt like my soul had meshed with his and that we were connected somehow. I poured my heart into the kiss, pushing farther until I felt his hands gently tugging on mine. Gradually, I pulled away and lowered my hands from his face. I was breathing heavily and he was looking at me more shocked than I had ever seen him. I could feel a blush creep into my cheeks and I was immediately embarrassed. Had I really just forced him to kiss me? I wasn't shy but that was brazen even for me. No knowing what to say I tucked my hair behind my ear. Saving me the anguish, he spoke first.

"You're right. We aren't friends. The last I checked, friends didn't kiss each other like that."

His eyebrow was raised as if in question as he stood casually in my room. I didn't understand how he could be so calm. My insides were churning and I couldn't believe he had been so unaffected by the kiss. I lowered my gaze to the floor as I spoke in a small voice. "I'm sorry....I don't know why I did that."

He reached out and tilted my head up to look at him and I saw his mouth quirk up on one side.

"Sophie, don't apologize. I know why you did it and soon you will too."

Not really knowing what that meant and not wanting to ask, I just smiled. He cocked his head to the side as if, he could hear something I didn't and then leaned forward to place a kiss on my forehead. I heard him softly say "I have to go now love. Get some rest. You are going to need it. You'll make the right choice, I have faith in you. "

Before I could respond, I felt a whoosh of air and then he was gone. I turned and ran to look out the window but I didn't see him there either. Sighing, I shut the window and crawled into bed. No matter how confused I was, I did need the rest.

The next morning, I woke with a sense of dread. It was the day, June 5th. I had until 11:00pm to find a way to stop Cassian and I didn't have a clue as to where to begin. I rolled out of bed and dressed quickly. I didn't know what I was going to do but I knew somewhere to figure it out.

On my way out of the house I scrawled a quick note to mom who had already left for work. I told her I was going swimming at the lake with friends and that I didn't know when I would be home. I really hoped she would never find out anything to say different.

I drove to the lake feeling sort of numb. I just knew if I could get there I could figure everything out. I had cut it pretty close to the wire but I was going to make a decision and soon. Once I reached the lake I hopped out of my car and started my walk along the bank. With no one else around, it was so peaceful. The only sounds I could hear were birds singing, the water lapping at the bank and my own feet crunching as I walked.

I knew I had come to the right place. I began to turn everything over in my mind. I knew I was going to have to face Cassian and although that scared the hell out of me, I decided my best bet was to wait for him to come to me. I had no idea where he was or how to find him but I knew he would have to come to Splendor Rock to perform his spell. I would wait for him there.

With that settled, I moved onto the biggest question I had yet to answer, who to choose to help me. On one hand I had Lucas, who claimed his love for me and I genuinely cared about. On the other, I had Daire, Who stirred something within in me that I didn't understand. One of them was a fake and I had no way of telling which one. I thought back over everything that had happened with each of them, all the way back to the night of my attack. Turning it all over, I made my decision.

I didn't understand why it had taken me so long to figure it out. The choice really was simple. I turned and headed back to my car, my heart lighter than it had been in a long while. Just knowing I had chosen and that I wasn't in this alone was a relief. The only thing I had to worry about then was if my powers would be enough to stop Cassian and the longer I thought on it the more confident I was. I was going to succeed or die trying. When I reached my car again, my spirits were up and I hopped in to go find my accomplice.

CHAPTER 16

I had cranked my car and began backing out of my space in the gravel lot when a thought struck me. I threw the vehicle in park and hopped out. I ran to the tree line and stood hands on my hips.

"Daire! I know you're in there! Come out!"

I waited a few beats a hearing nothing I yelled again. "I mean it! This isn't the time to play games. You have been spying on me all this time and you expect me to think today is any different? I don't think so! Now, bring your butt out here!"

My voice was full of annoyance and I was glad there was no one else at the lake. Anyone walking by would have thought I was crazy, yelling at trees.
I sucked in a deep breath, preparing to yell again when I heard the brush in the trees rustle. Then he stepped out into the open and I was shocked. His clothes were tattered and his normally pristine appearance was haggard. There were even large rips down the front of his jeans. Not thinking twice, I rushed forward.
"Oh my god! Are you okay? What happened to you?"

He put his hands up and caught me by the shoulders bringing me to a halt. He smiled as he spoke.

"No worries, Blondie...I'll clean up. Now, that you have yelled at me would you mind telling me why?"

He released my shoulders and not seeing any wounds on him I resisted the urge to inspect him.

"Oh...I wanted you to know that I have made my decision."

He looked at me expectantly. I looked at the ground not sure of the words to answer with. In the sandy dirt, I noticed a sliver of broken glass and I knew what to do. I leaned down and picked it up and then looking straight into his eyes, I tilted my head and made a small nick in my throat. It stung with pain but I knew I had only cut deep enough for blood to flow. His nostrils flared and I could see that his fangs had appeared. Without hesitation, I cocked my head to the side and offered my neck to him. He crooked his finger under my chin and made me look at him again, then he leaned forward and brushed a gentle kiss over my mouth and then another over my cheek and then another and another until he had traveled down to my neck. I braced myself for the pain I knew was going to come. My body was rigid as he wrapped his arms around me and then I felt him bite. I felt two small stings and then the pain was gone. The only thing I felt was his lips on my skin and the gentle motion of his tongue as he sucked. Wrapping my arms around him, I leaned my body into his and waited. It was the most intimate situation I had ever been in. I felt empowered even though I was giving some of my actual powers away. I knew I wouldn't regret my decision. After a moment, He pulled away, I could see that his fangs were still out and tinged pink as he spoke. "That's enough. Can you heal yourself?"

"I don't know. I can try." Not having tried to heal myself before, I was skeptical that I would be able to do it but I closed my eyes and focused all my thoughts on the wound. I felt a familiar warmth flow through me and concentrate on my throat. After a moment, I opened my eyes and looked into his.

"Did it work?" I asked questioningly.
He nodded. "Yes, it worked."

I let out a breath of relief. With our moment of closeness over, I was unsure of what to say to him, but I knew I needed to say it fast. I was running out of time before I had to face Cassian and I didn't want to charge in without a plan. He must have picked up on my thoughts because he said "Don't worry little love, I'll help you."

I smiled, feeling much better knowing that I wouldn't be alone. His eyes scanned my face as if searching for something and then he spoke again. "Why did you choose me?"

He had been so sure that I would choose him before that I was surprised by his question.

"Not once since we met, have you lied to me, even when I didn't want the truth. You may not tell me everything but you don't lie."

He nodded as if expecting my answer, and when I stopped he gave me a questioning stare. His usual arrogant tone was back when he spoke. "That's the only reason?"

I sucked in a deep breath. He was right. It wasn't the only reason.

"Not exactly. I did choose you because you don't lie but my grandmother also told me to follow my heart. I have never been in love and I don't know if I am but I know that love is supposed to be something you fight for. You're not supposed to run when it gets hard. If Lucas loved me like he says he does he would fight for what we had. The differences between us wouldn't matter. Love requires effort from both sides and instead of doing that, he ran. I might care about him but knowing that he could let me go that easy, I could never give him my whole heart. Then there is you, I don't know what this is between us and you do a lot of things I don't like but I know that I am willing to fight to find out. Are you?"

163

His face was blank as he stood staring at me. Then, without saying anything he stepped forward and brushed a kiss to my forehead. I heard him softly say "Yes. I don't know why but I am."

Taking a step back from me, he had his grin in place and our personal moment broken, said "You ready to make a plan, Blondie?"
I nodded and spoke "First, do you want to explain why you're all torn up?"

I waited for his answer but he only stood, silently. Realizing he wasn't going to answer, I gently took his hand and held it.

"You said you were willing to fight with me, which means being up front with me. We are in this together and if you're not telling me everything, we aren't going to make it very far."

He slowly nodded and stepped forward, wrapping his arms around me and burying my face into his chest. I hadn't been expecting him to hug me and then I realized that my feet were no longer on the ground and his grip was tight around me. I felt the air whoosh around us and realized we must be flying. Then, abruptly, the air stopped flowing and I felt solid ground beneath my feet. Keeping his hands on me to make sure I was steady, he stepped back. Not recognizing my surrounding I started a slow turn to inspect everything.

We were in an apartment. I could tell from the brick walls that the building was historic but all of the furnishings were modern. One wall was covered by large arched windows covered in black drapes. To the right was a red brick wall with a fireplace that had a flat screen T.V. centered above it. The floors were dark wood and there was a black area rug with intricate red swirls sitting under a modern black leather couch and love seat in front of the fireplace. There was a dark wood coffee table situated in the center and two massive bookshelves one each side of the fireplace. A door off to the side had locks on it and I could guess that it was the way out. Continuing my turn I saw the kitchen. It was small but beautiful. It had dark granite countertops and all stainless steel appliances. Off side of the kitchen, sat a small wooden dinette set with seating for four and looking behind it I could see a door that was cracked far enough to reveal a bathroom. Having made almost a full circle I was again facing Daire. His expression was hesitant as I spoke. "Do you live here?"

His voice was matter of fact when he spoke "Yes, you wanted me to up front, so I am. Also, I needed a change of clothes."

While talking, he turned and walked toward a door in the living area. It was partially hidden from view by one of the books cases and I had missed on my initial survey but I realized it must be his bedroom. Not wanting to intrude, I didn't follow. Instead, I walked over to the couch and sat down leaning back into the cool leather. It wasn't even noon and I was tired. After sitting in silence for a moment, Daire came back into the room and I was speechless.

He was standing in the doorway, wearing nothing but a pair of dark wash jeans. They sat low on his hips and I could glimpse the top band of his boxers. His shirtless form was a flawless creamy white and I could see defined muscles in his chest and shoulders. He was beautiful. Realizing my mouth had dropped open, I quickly clamped it shut and dropped my eyes to the floor. Then, I heard him laugh for the first time. It was a deep and wonderful sound. His body had been magnificent but his laugh was even more so. Chancing a glance at him, I saw him pull a t-shirt over his head as he said "You did say not to hide things from you."

I couldn't hide the smile that crept across my face as he walked over the love seat across from me and sat. He rested one of his arms across the back of the couch as he leaned back, looking relaxed. He looked at me and said "Alright, ask your questions."
Barely knowing where to begin I asked "Where are we and how did we get here?"

He answered with "We're still in Splendor. This is my apartment and you should know it well considering it's on your way home from the coffee shop. As for how we got here, it's called

166

transporting and it's something most vampires can do as they age and gain power."

Thinking over my route home from The Drip, I could remember only one building that could have and apartment. It was a three story brick building and it was right off the square. It would have been only yards from where I first met Daire. Not liking the memory of that night, I pushed it away and concentrated on transporting. I had never heard of it but I knowing I had a lot to learn about the supernatural and more pressing matters to deal with, I resisted the urge to launch into questions on it. Instead, I said "What happened to you earlier? Why were you all torn up?"

 I could see the hesitation on his face as he answered. "I had a small run in with a few goblins." I waited a beat for him to elaborate but when he didn't I pushed forward. "Why?"
With a sigh, he said "I encountered them near your house last night after I left you. Don't worry, I took care of it." His eyes scanned my face for my reaction.

My heart started pounding and I asked a question I already knew the answer to. "My house? Why?"

His voice was matter of fact as he said "I didn't take the time to ask but I'm sure they were working for Cassian. He probably sent them to make sure you didn't interfere."

My throat felt like it was closing up and my chest grew tight. "What about my family? I can't believe I never thought of this before, they could be in danger! How could I be so stupid?"

I was angry with myself for not having thought of the possibility before. I had assumed that Cassian would leave me alone since he couldn't harm me until after the spell and I never even thought that he could use my family against me. I jumped up from the couch headed toward the door.

Before I could make it more than two steps, Daire appeared in front of me and grabbed me by the shoulders. "They are fine. I enthralled you're mother into taking a spontaneous vacation to see your grandmother in Florida. Bailey is with her. You'll have to forgive her for not leaving a note."

As his words sank in, relief settled in me. I wrapped my arms around him and hugged him. I was beyond grateful for what he had done. I didn't know how I would ever repay him. Words would never be enough, so I only mumbled a "thank you."

Instead of acknowledging me, he pulled away and went back to sit. I took my place across from him as he said "Now that your questions are answered, what do you plan to do about Cassian?"

Still a little shaky over the fear I had felt for my mom and Bailey, I said "I thought I could wait for him at Splendor Rock. I don't know how to find him but I know he'll be there."

He raised a brow skeptically as he said "You have a lot to learn. Cassian is very old, one of the first of our kind. Being so old makes him very powerful. He would know you were there the minute he arrived. Also, I would imagine he is already there and if not he is nearby. He'll be preparing for tonight. I think you need a new plan."

I hadn't even thought about the fact that my plan might be flawed so I had no idea where to go from there. I said "What do you suggest then?"

"I say we arrive right before 11:00. I'll transport us there. With any luck we'll surprise him. He'll be on guard though, so he may be ready. It's a chance we are going to have to take."

Accepting his plan, I nodded. Looking into my eyes he asked "Are you sure you trust me to handle the plan? It's your life after all."

I only nodded. I had given him my blood and if he was untrustworthy I was already in trouble.

He nodded back and said "Alright, how are your powers? I saw your little pyrotechnic show in your backyard but to defeat Cassian you are going to need a lot more than that."

I shook my head knowing I shouldn't be surprised that he had been watching. Still shaking my head I said "I don't know, I haven't used them much since then."

I saw his face flash with anger as he responded. "How foolish could you be?! You knew what was coming, yet you did nothing to prepare. Do you have a death wish? I certainly don't but since I am in this with you I might as well resign myself to one!"

I could almost feel his anger and guilt settled into me. I hadn't even thought about the fact that I could endanger someone other than myself. My voice broke as I spoke. "No…I…I just wanted to be normal. I didn't ask for any of this and it was driving me crazy! If I was going to die I wanted to experience as much normal as I could before it happened. I'm only 18 years old, why is it my responsibility to save people? I am supposed to be making plans to go to college; Instead, I am worried about dying! I don't understand why it all falls on me!"

I saw the anger on his face subside as my eyes started tearing up and he spoke "Blondie, you're not normal if there even is a such thing and you need to accept that. If you can't embrace what you are, facing Cassian is pointless."

I knew what he said was true but it I couldn't just let go of who I used to be. Even if I survived the night my life was never going to be the same and it scared me. I used to know who I was but with this newfound power, how could I be the same person? I nodded to acknowledge him as I said "I know. I'm sorry. I could practice now?"

He replied with "No. You need all the strength you can get for tonight. If you practice it will make you weak and I can see that you are already tired."

He was right, I could feel my eyelids drooping and my limbs felt heavy. I saw him get up and skirt the coffee table to come stand in front of me. He leaned down and scooped me up off the couch. Surprised, I locked my arms around his neck to hold on. Before I could ask what he was doing he had walked into his bedroom.
It was a simple but elegant space with only a large black chair and matching ottoman in one corner, an ornate dresser and a huge wooden bed with a black canopy. The canopy was tied back and I could see the comforter and pillows were deep red and very plush. It suited him perfectly.
He walked to the side of the bed and holding me with one arm pulled the blankets back and laid me on its softness. I shot him a confused look but he ignored me and reached down to pull off my tennis

shoes. I thought about objecting but this behavior was so strange for him that I kept quiet. He pulled the covers over me and walked to the lone window in the room, closing the dark curtains as he said "Get some rest, you'll need it. I'll wake you in a while."

He then walked out, shutting the door behind him. I lay in the dark turning the morning over in my mind. Daire's behavior had been so strange. Guilt started to eat at me when I realized that the whole time I had known him, I thought that he was unfeeling but I was wrong. He had feelings, he just hid them deep down inside of himself. Why he did was a mystery to me but I promised myself that if I survived, I was going to find out. With that, I sunk into sleep.

A gentle brush over my cheek woke me. I opened my eyes and was confused at my surroundings. Blinking my eyes, the morning came rushing back to me. Looking up, I saw Daire seated on the edge of the bed. My voice was still sleepy as I asked "what time is it?"

"Just after seven."

I shot up to a sitting position. I had slept for almost seven hours. Daire rose from the bed giving me room to get up. Once on my feet, I spoke. "Sorry. I didn't mean to sleep so long."

"You needed the rest. I would imagine you haven't been sleeping well."

He was right about that. He turned and headed out of the door into the living room and I followed behind him. As worried as I was about Cassian, I was surprised at how comfortable I was feeling. I never pictured that I would feel secure enough with Daire to sleep in his bed. There were so many things about him that I had yet to learn but I knew I was safe with him. Stepping into the living area, I could smell food and my stomach gurgled. I hadn't eaten anything earlier in the day and I was regretting it. Glancing at the kitchen area, I saw Daire pick up a plate from the counter and he motioned me toward the dining table. As I made it to the table and sat down, he placed the plate in front of me and I could see that it was filled with chocolate chip pancakes already slathered in syrup. I smiled, it was one of my favorite foods and I wasn't surprised that he would know that. I was surprised that he knew how to cook. He took a seat across from me as I asked "Did you make these?"

His smile reached his eyes as he answered. "Do you doubt my abilities? I assure you they are safe to eat."

I gave a giggle and said "No, I was just curious since, you don't eat. I assumed you wouldn't ever have had a reason to learn."

173

Still smiling, he nodded but didn't say anything other than "Eat. You must be hungry and you need the energy."

I picked up my fork and started eating. I felt a little self-conscious as he watched me. I thought about making conversation but I was so hungry that I decided eating was a better option. He seemed content to watch me until he rose and made his way into the bedroom. I finished off the pancakes and walked into the kitchen and washed my plate. Not knowing where to put it, I set it on the counter and made my way into the living room and sat down on the couch. Daire came back into the room and I watched him as he sat down next to me on the couch. He held out his arm and without hesitation, I curled into his side. Knowing we would have to leave soon, I said what was on my mind.

"Daire?"

"Yes?"

"I really hope we make it out of this tonight. I don't know what this is between us but I know that I want to find out."

There was a pause and then I heard him say "Don't worry love, it'll all be alright."

I took strength from his words and curled into his side tighter. We sat in silence. Daire seemed to

understand that I didn't need words; I only needed
the comfort of having him hold me. My confidence
started to grow as we sat there. Now that I had
seen this whole other side of Daire, I knew I made
the right decision in choosing him. I didn't know if
what I felt for him was love but I was pretty sure it
could be someday. Before that morning I had
resigned myself to dying. I loved my family and I
loved Nora but I knew that if anything happened to
me that they would eventually move past it. They
were all strong people and I had every faith that
they could make it okay without me. I could admit
that I had given up before I even got started but
sitting with Daire I had a renewed determination. I
wanted to know what was between us and I wasn't
giving it up without a fight. I may not be normal but I
had a right to experience love. Love is something
that anybody can have if they are willing to fight for
it and I was. I had said that Lucas couldn't love me
if he was willing to give me up and I believed that. I
wasn't giving up on Daire. I looked up at him, my
voice firm when I spoke. "We have two hours until
we have to be at the lake. I need to know every
possible way to kill a vampire and we need to
gather anything we might need."

He smiled down at me in return and simply
answered with "Took you long enough."

CHAPTER 17

Standing in my bedroom, I took a deep breath and looked around making sure I hadn't forgotten anything. Daire stood leaned against the doorjamb watching me with a smile. We had been over every possible way to kill and vampire and Daire had given me a silver dagger that would do the job. Apparently, Lucas had left out a few things during my vampires 101 course. I was worried about what that meant. I knew he must not be what he seemed since I had chosen Daire but I was hoping Lucas wasn't involved with Cassian. With no time to dwell on it, I buried the thoughts and started toward Daire, tucking the sheathed dagger into my back pocket.

He straightened as he said. "Ready, Blondie?"

I still didn't have a solid plan but it was minutes until 11:00 and I didn't have time for anything else. I was as prepared as I was going to get. I nodded and he stepped forward to wrap his arms around me. I closed my eyes and felt the familiar flying sensation of transporting and then my feet were on solid ground. With a finger to his lips, Daire stepped back from me. I knew we were just inside the tree line by Splendor Rock but the darkness of the woods made it difficult to make anything out. Daire took my hand and pointed toward a bush. Silently, I crept over to look through its branches. On the other side, I could see Splendor Rock jutting out over the lake and right in front of it was a large fire. I could make out Cassian standing beside it and he was chanting, wearing a long robe. Off to the side I could see what appeared to be two goblins and….Lucas. My heart sank. I hadn't chosen him but I did care about him and seeing him there I knew that I had been used. We were supposed to be friends and he betrayed me. I felt a gentle squeeze on my hand and I knew Daire knew what I was thinking. Pushing that all away, I knew I had to act. I took a deep breath and I sprang through the bushes. A few yards away Cassian turned and I threw my hand out in front of me, fire shooting out of it. In one long stream in came to an end at Cassian. For a split second I was excited. All I had to do was keep him burning long enough and it would be over. Then I realized that he wasn't burning at all. It was like there was a force field around him, stopping the flames mere inches from him. I heard a thud beside me and glancing over I realized that Daire had come through right after me and he was struggling with one of the goblins. The other lay on the ground and was already melting into a black puddle. It was then that I noticed Lucas creeping up behind Daire, gripping a wooden stake. He glanced up at me and gave a rueful expression and then he lunged forward. With no time to think, I threw my hand towards him and released the fire. He stumbled back but just like Cassian, he didn't burn. Not knowing what to next, I looked over at Daire in time to see him twist the goblins neck. I heard a sickening crunch and the creature fell forward onto the ground. Daire looked up at me and I could see that his fangs were out and his cheek was cut but he seemed otherwise unharmed. I was turning my attention back to Lucas when I felt myself rising up off the ground. The flames from my hands died as I floated upward. I tried to turn but suspended off the ground, it was useless. Just like my last encounter with Cassian, I couldn't move or speak. I saw Daire float up across from me as I heard the bone chilling voice that I would never forget.

"Sophie, you've been nothing but trouble for me."

As he spoke he came to stand between Daire and me. I met his black eyes with mine, refusing to show fear.

He continued speaking "I would kill you now if you didn't have to be alive for this spell to work."

He looked over at Lucas who was still standing a few yards away and he motioned him over. As Lucas obeyed he turned his attention back to me and spoke again. "How do you like my Lucas? How does it feel to know that he has worked for me all along? That everything between you was a lie?"

As he said those words Lucas called out "NO! Don't listen to him!"

Cassian Hissed. "Lucas, remember our deal. Shut your mouth or you get nothing!"

Lucas immediately turned his gaze to the ground and stopped talking. With Lucas quiet, Cassian turned to me again. "I have known about you since you were born. I have spent all this time waiting for today. Your grandmother locked up my love and you will pay for it."

I saw Daire who was still suspended, helpless in the air; suddenly drop to ground with a thud. He was in his feet quickly and charging at Cassian almost faster than my eyes could follow but before he could reach him Cassian reached into the folds of his robe and turned. I saw a glint of silver fly through the air and land in Daire's chest. Daire stumbled backwards and fell to the ground, not moving. I could see the handle of a dagger protruding from his chest. Cassian turned back to give me a wicked smile, while Lucas stood, seemingly in shock.

I heard Cassian's icy voice wash over me, full of hate. "Now dear Sophie, you'll suffer like I did…until I kill you."

Having said that he didn't spare me another glance as he walked past me and resumed his chanting around the fire. Seeing Daire still motionless on the ground, something inside me snapped. I realized that Daire was probably dead and I had never felt so much anger in my life. How could he take him away from me? I could feel my insides churning and I pushed against the magic holding me with everything I had. When nothing happened, I pushed harder. I could still hear Cassian's chanting but then I heard a new sound. It was the sound of rain. Looking in front of me, I could see the rain sweeping down the shoreline of the lake and then it was on us. It was a pouring rain that fell like a blanket, covering everything. I continued pushing and suddenly, I was free. I fell to my knees as I dropped to the now muddy ground. I turned toward Cassian and through the sheet of rain, I could see that his fire was almost out and he had rage on his face. Without a second's hesitation, I focused my thoughts on him and all I hoped for was pain. I wanted him to hurt the way I did. He started toward me but after two steps he doubled over. He seemed to be gasping for air as he finally fell all the way to the ground. I walked up to him without any fear. Reaching for the Dagger in my back pocket, I was going to kill him and I wasn't going to feel any remorse. It's what he deserved. Standing over him, dagger in hand, I realized that if I killed him, I wouldn't be any better than he was. He wanted to kill me out of revenge and killing him for what he did to Daire would make me evil too. Over the last few months, I had been so afraid that having powers made me somebody different but it didn't. Having powers might change my life but it could only change me if I let it. Making a decision, I dropped the dagger into the mud and focused all of my thoughts on Cassian and Splendor Rock. Still writing in pain, he lifted from the ground, floated to the rock and lay flat against the side of it. I watched as the rock seemed to grow over him. In a few seconds you couldn't see him at all, he had been completely engulfed, stuck forever. I should have felt relief but I didn't. I turned and ran to Daire's body. He was still lying motionless as before. As I reached him and kneeled into the mud, the rain stopped and the light of the full moon cascaded over him. I gripped the dagger handle with both hands and pulled it out of his chest. Feeling the metal slide out of him made me nauseous. Looking at his face, seeing it so blank I could feel the tears well in my eyes and a sob building in my chest. As I lifted his head to cradle it in my lap, I felt a hand lay gently on my shoulder. I looked up to see Lucas standing over me and I filled with anger.

"DON'T TOUCH ME! You helped do this! Get away!"

Lucas pulled his hand away and stepped back.

"Sophie I'm sorry. I wish you could understand, I never meant to hurt you but no matter how much you want him back, it's over. He's gone."

A sob escaped me and I shouted at him "GO AWAY !"

As Lucas's words sank in, something Daire had said to me came flooding back. When I told him I

181

couldn't levitate myself, he had said "You didn't want it bad enough" I knew now that he was right but I knew something I did want. Completely disregarding Lucas, I leaned over Daire and placed my hand on his chest. I focused everything I had on him and willed him to heal. When nothing seemed to happen, I poured everything I had into it. I don't know how long I sat there but I refused to give up. Finally, I could feel myself growing tired and the edges of my vision started to blur. Refusing to give in, I stared at his face and kept pushing. My head started to swim and I could feel myself growing faint. I struggled not to, but I could feel myself falling to the side. I closed my eyes and gave in. I felt a hand catch me before I hit the ground and then my world went black.

CHAPTER 18

I cracked my eyelids and was blinded by bright
light. Painfully, I blinked rapidly in confusion. I was
in Daire's room. Adrenaline coursed through me
and I shot up out of the bed and ran into the living
area of the apartment. As I skidded to a stop in the
doorway, I saw Daire standing in the middle of the
large room looking straight at me and before I could
think I ran across the room and launched myself at
him. It seemed too good to be true. He was alive!
He raised his arms and caught me effortlessly. With
his arms wrapped around me, he spun me in a
circle, my feet never touching the ground. As we
made the full turn he sat me on my feet and looked
down at me to speak "I wondered how long you
were going to sleep." I was smiling so big my
cheeks hurt as I responded. "Who cares how long I
slept! You're alive!"

"Returning my smile he said "Yes, thanks to you.
Now, why don't you tell me everything I missed?"

He could have asked me anything and I would have
agreed to it. So I spent the morning relaying
everything he had missed from the night before.
When I was finished telling him everything he
looked at me and said "I owe you my life. Nothing I
do for you will ever measure up to that."

I shook my head and said "It doesn't have to. Although, there is something I'd like you to do for me."

He gave me a skeptical look as he said "What is it that you want?"

"Do you think you could go to the lake with me today? I'd like to go buy my house and change clothes first but I have always loved it there and I don't want it ruined for me."

Nodding in understanding he said "As you wish" as he wrapped his arms around me.

Later, we walked down in the lake's shoreline in silence. Daire had transported us and I could see Splendor Rock in the distance. The day was so beautiful it was hard to imagine that the night before had actually taken place here. As we neared the rock I was surprised at how happy I was. I was afraid the night before had ruined the lake for me but we were both alive and that was something worth being happy about. As we reached the rock, I studied it in place at the water's edge. It looked the same as it always had. I looked around at the ground but I saw nothing to prove that the night before had happened. It was the same sandy shoreline it had always been. Daire had told me that after I had collapsed he had transported me to his apartment and then came back to clean up the scene. I was glad that he had taken care of it; it was a relief not to have to see it again. Daire stood a few yards away, watching me. I looked up at him and voiced a question that had been nagging me all morning. "I thought my blood was supposed to give you power but it didn't seem to make you any stronger or powerful than you already were."

He was nodding as he answered "I have had the same thought. I didn't feel any different. I don't know what that means but if you want we'll try to find out."

I shook my head yes. I didn't know if the blood didn't work because we did something wrong or because we hadn't needed it to but I wanted to know why. My voice was hesitant as I voiced another question "Did you... did you see Lucas last night?"
Daire shook his head. "No, when I came to, there was only the two of us here."

I sighed. I didn't know what had happened to him but I hoped he was alright. He had lied to me but I still couldn't believe he ever wanted to hurt me. Daire's voice cut into my thoughts. "You told me why you chose me to help you but what made you decide to give things between us a try?"

I took a deep breath. I had asked myself the same question and I knew he deserved an explanation but I wasn't sure how he would handle it. "I was so worried about the things you did that I was afraid of what caring for you meant. You kill people, Daire and I was afraid that being with you would make me a horrible person. Then, I realized that it was my choice. Just like with Cassian, I can only become an awful person if I let myself. My choices are what matter, not anyone else's."

I searched his face for a reaction. I had basically called him a horrible person but it was the truth and after everything he had done for me, he deserved that. His eyes met mine and I braced myself as he started to speak. "I think there are some things I need to explain. I..."
His voice trailed off and his face showed absolute shock. I quickly realized that his attention wasn't on me anymore but instead he was looking at something over my shoulder. Slowly turning around, I saw her. She was standing at the edge of the trees and she was beautiful. Her long wavy hair was chestnut brown and she wore a white flowing dress. Her face had defined bones and was set off by oddly, familiar gray eyes. She met my gaze head on as she started to speak "Well, hello Sophie!"

Confused that she would know my name I said "Who are you?"

She laughed as I asked and it was a cold and hollow sound. Instinctively, I started backing up toward Daire. Chancing a glance, behind me I saw Daire still standing, straight and not moving. His face was blank. Turning my eyes back to the stranger I heard her say "My name is Emily. You know my brother."

As her words sank in, I realized that she was Lucas's sister. He had been sure that she was dead. As I tried to find an explanation for her being here, she started coming toward Daire, gliding over the ground as if she was floating, her long dress flowing behind her. I stepped to the side out of her path, not wanting her to get close to me. I saw her glide up to Daire who was still standing blank and rigid. She stopped inches in front of him and with a cruel smile on her face, I heard her say "Hello, Maker."

7028691R00105

Printed in Great Britain
by Amazon.co.uk, Ltd.,
Marston Gate.